ASBURY HIGH

AND THE

THIEF'S GAMBLE

Hi!
 This is a first edition,
which has recently been
republished. If you enjoyed
leave a review on Amazon
 and Goodreads!

Kelly Brady Channick

PURPLEMILKPUBLISHING

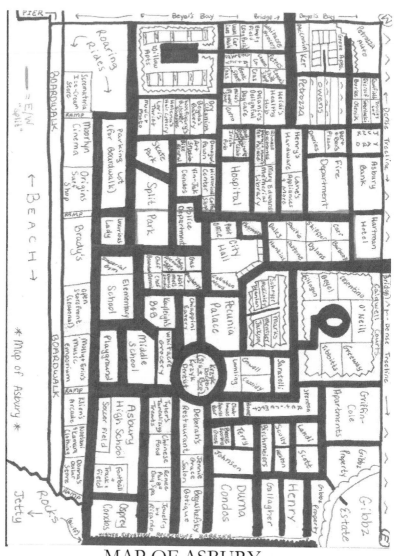

MAP OF ASBURY

DEDICATION

I dedicate this book to the love of my life, and number one
fan, Ryan Channick. You give me the courage to turn my
dreams into a reality.

Asbury High and the Thief's Gamble © Copyright 2019
Kelly Brady Channick

For more information, email: kbchannick@gmail.com

Editor: Alexandra Beyda, Esq.

Cover Designed by: Susan Schafer of Happy Artist Publishers

Created by: Purple Milk Publishing

ISBN: 978-1-7343073-0-6

ASBURY HIGH AND THE THIEF'S GAMBLE

CONTENTS

ACKNOWLEDGMENTS

As with any good story, more than one voice is needed to tell it.

First and foremost, I would like to thank my incredible husband again. Ryan, your encouragement and never-ending love has turned my dream into a reality. I could not have made this book, or this life, happen without you.

To Dennis and Donna Brady, or dad and mom. Other than giving me life, thank you for raising me to value creativity, hard-work, and strength; and thank you for teaching me that it is far better to stand out than to fit in.

To my two crazy, smart, and good-looking sisters. Diz and Shanski, thank you for giving me a lifetime of humor and inspiration, as well as plenty of unique memories to shape into stories.

To my Granny La, thank you for teaching me to read and to laugh. You're a legend!

To my grandparents down in Florida, Edward and Mary Cassidy. Thank you for the endless love and resounding positivity.

To my bonus grandparents, Dolly and Michael Petrozza. Thank you for always being there for me, from birthdays to NCAA playoff games. Mr. P, sorry I waited so long to finish, but I know you're reading your own copy of Asbury High up in heaven.

To my lifetime guardian angel, my grandpa, Edward Brady. I wish I could've known you, but I know you'd be proud and are probably reading this alongside Mr. P---after playing a game on one on one, of course.

To my second family, Brandan, Lynn, Catherine, Carly and Owen Dierolf. Thank you for inspiring me and filling my life with joy.

To my Aunt Lori, thank you for encouraging my writing, and supplying my life with color.

To my brother-in-law, Steve. Thank you for all of those times you watched my (BIG) little guy, so I could get some work done! You are more helpful than you'll ever know.

To my amazing in-laws, Steven and Deborah Channick. Thank you for giving me your son, and for always cheering on my every endeavor.

To my sister-in-law Christy Channick. Thank you for your continual support and artistic personality.

To Kurt Channick, thank you for always dropping some new knowledge on me --- and all the encouragement you always provide.

To my wonderful, multi-talented Editor, Alexandra Beyda, thank you for your scrutiny. And thanks for always being there to answer legal questions--- you're a (good-looking) walking law book.

To my awesome, computer-savvy brother-in law, Todd Channick. Thank you for crafting such an amazing website.

To my cover illustrator, book designer, and trusted advisor, Susan Schafer. Thank you, everything you do comes out as beautiful as you are.

And finally, they say the best things come in threes:

To my two dogs and cat, Dexter, Maui and Donnie. You guys may be crazy, but you're the absolute cure for writer's block.

To my childhood best friends--- Dana Cosentino, Catherine & Carly Dierolf and Sarah Gibbs. Thank you for encouraging my weirdness and always letting me make up the rules and games... and thanks for your names!

To my three favorite teachers of all time--- who have probably never gotten the credit they deserve: **Mr. David Jackson,** my unforgettable and exceedingly clever fourth and fifth grade teacher. Thank you for believing in me at such a young age and going above and beyond to instill the value of imagination. To **Mrs. Michelle Forsman,** my goofy and creative eighth grade teacher. Thank you for dedicating your time to make learning memorable and fun, and helping me craft my passion for writing. And, to my hilarious and wise twelfth grade English teacher, **Ms. Geralyn Williscroft.** Thank you for motivating me to do what I love best... and editing all of my written college assignments. It goes without saying that you've all shaped more lives than you realize, and I hope your students appreciate your worth.

1

If a stranger to Asbury was to ask, "Who's the craziest driver around?", nobody would hesitate to answer: Eddie. Driving a bus in the coastal town of Asbury isn't a job to be taken lightly. Naturally, Eddie knew the job consisted of maneuvering through hurricanes and around shoobies (tourists with both zero driving skills and no common sense). Add to that his daredevil driving and foolhardy feats, and Eddie was cemented in his title. In fact, it's rumored that Eddie drove through flood waters---twelve feet deep--- just to tell his mother that dinner at his house was canceled. And it's common knowledge that Eddie can make an eighteen-wheeler do a full 1080 (yes, ten-eighty), without breaking a sweat. With his reputation established as the zaniest driver around, there was nothing, and nobody, in Asbury that could rival the infamous Eddie.

That being stated, the wily bus driver had to slam on the brakes as a sleek limo sped past his bus, toward the high school. Even though Eddie blared his horn several times, the limo seemed not to care and accelerated away. Inside the lustrous limo, Cornelious couldn't suppress a groan, and successfully cut off his father's 'new school, new friends' speech.

"Taking a limo the first day of school isn't exactly being inconspicuous, sir."

"Well, that's exactly the point my boy. As a Gibbz you need to stand out and always make an entrance," beamed Jeremiah Gibbz as he sat across from his son and appraised his good looks. "Being a governor's son, and heir to billions will turn a lot of heads. You have hung out with those three miscreants for the past seven years and I believe it's time for an upgrade."

"Miscreants?" The word always made Cornelious laugh out loud, which he also always instantly regretted. Clearly, Jeremiah Gibbz, standing at six feet five inches, was not one for laughing matters. As governor and heir to old-time money, everything had to be classified and categorized, including his only child. Besides money, Jeremiah Gibbz highly treasured appearances. To jumpstart his day, Jeremiah kept a strict diet and underwent a two-hour workout regimen from four to six each morning. Other than ensuring each muscle in his body was sculpted and intact, Jeremiah was sure to always look his best---and nine times out of ten that meant formalwear. But perhaps his most intimidating trait was his steel-gray eyes, which never seem to lose their glare, even when (on rare occasions) he smiled.

Evidently not smiling, Jeremiah continued, "You think your future is funny? You think this is a JOKE?! Hmmph! It may very well be if you don't get your act together!"

"Sorry, sir," mumbled Cornelious, as the limo stopped abruptly in front of the grand Asbury High.

****

People often say high school is where you meet your real friends; or that once you enter high school, cliques will separate you from your grade school buddies. Maddie mused over this idea as she laced up her worn-out high-top Converses and hopped off Eddie's bus, glad to make it to Asbury High in one piece. Pulling back her thick, unruly, brown hair into a tight ponytail, Maddie looked up at the humongous four-story, brick-built Asbury High. With a shiny, golden dome topping it off, it seemed to boast of greatness, while warning surrounding schools to give up any attempt at competition. Although no real kid ever dreams of going to school (except that one weirdo in every grade), Asbury is pretty much a dream school. Located right off the boardwalk, Asbury High is basically a beachfront property. Maddie had even heard, from reliable sources, that some classes were held on the beach itself! And other than its beautiful location, Maddie was overjoyed that the soccer field was situated behind the school (beachside), as the fresh air and ocean breeze cooled her down immensely during the past few weeks' intense preseason.

Mulling it over, the math was clearly not in her favor--the school's population consisted of East Asbury or richie riches: 62%, and West Asbury or wrong side of the tracks: 38%, which was where she happened to fall. But no matter, because Maddie knew she had luck on her side when she moved to Asbury back in the second grade. Maddie grinned as she remembered walking into Mr. Burke's class knowing virtually nobody. Some kids, aka big-blonde-bully Jonas Butters or JB, thought it was funny that poor little red-headed Pilot couldn't afford a lunch. Maddie was about to stand up to JB, when a spunky little blonde girl named Carly Cosentino, went up to Pilot and gave him her lunch, saying she wasn't hungry and told JB to 'shove it.'

Maddie found herself chuckling now, just as she couldn't help but laugh then. Back then, her laughter had caused everyone to look over strangely at the 'new kid,' and made her an automatic enemy of JB. Needless to say, Maddie joined Carly and Pilot for recess near the big yellow slide. Maddie had heard JB saying he was going to get Carly back (for his embarrassment), but Carly just shrugged it off and elected to play monkeys on the Jungle Gym. Right when Carly reached the peak of the Jungle Gym, JB scrambled up the backside and pushed Carly off of the top and onto the mulch, instantly breaking her wrist. Realizing the severity of her new friend's injury, Maddie stood up and punched JB square in the face.

Unexpectedly, JB got up fairly quickly, for he was quite big even back then, and shoved Maddie to the ground, cleverly retorting: "you shove it!"

Giving Maddie no time to get her bearings, JB roughly grabbed Maddie by the collar and raised his hand to strike her, but instead found himself tumbling backward. Maddie watched as a well-dressed, shaggy-haired kid came out of nowhere and tackled JB to ground. A small fight ensued but was quickly broken up by the frantic playground teachers.

"Well, I'm glad that's over," Maddie said as she rejoined Pilot and Carly, who were heading to the nurse.

"JB never forgets his enemies," JB hissed as he passed by them.

"JB also talks in third person, and wears his mom's underwear," the shaggy-haired kid laughed, catching up with the trio.

"That was one time, and my mom forgot to do the wash!" JB bellowed as he stormed off.

"I'm Cornelious," the shaggy-haired kid offered his hand to Maddie.

She smiled in return, "I like your style." Then, realizing how nicely dressed he was, "well, not your clothes but uh… I'm Maddie."

And voila! Our friendship was established and I couldn't be prouder! In fact, we've grown tighter than a bathing suit on Mrs. Simmons, Maddie reflected. Glancing up at the looming school before her, Maddie swallowed and thought that although her gang has begun to excel in different areas, they remained as close as ever---or at least she hoped so.

"Hey, Mad!" Maddie returned to the present as Carly yelled from the passenger seat of her older sister's car. Maddie cringed as Mia Cosentino whipped into the student lot and parked her baby blue convertible. "WHEW, Mia drives like a madman! She gives your bus driver a run for his money! Man, you sure got tan this summer, you make me look like a closet case!" Carly exclaimed as she ran over to Maddie and began jabbering a mile a minute about cheerleading tryouts, and her countless hours of preparation. Carly may be your regular old-fashioned, blonde-haired, blue-eyed, sweetest little girl next door, but don't let that fool you, remember how they met?

Maddie was about to comment on Mia's ride, when Carly suddenly interrupted the conversation, as they were joined by Pilot.

"Pilot! Oh, what happened to your hair?" Carly laughed as she tussled his erratic red hair.

"I didn't have time to brush it. In fact, I'm pretty sure someone stole it!" Pilot replied seriously.

"Someone stole what? Your brush?" Carly couldn't help but laugh, causing Maddie to join in as well.

Pilot Owens may have a weird name, crazy red hair, and wild green eyes, but he is a technological god. Unbeknownst to all, this summer he had successfully hacked into the Moorlyn theatre database and secured the gang free tickets for every movie premiere. Talk about a sweet deal!

"Look who's arriving in style this year," Pilot announced out of the blue.

Maddie looked over to see a tall, shaggy brown-haired boy with deep blue eyes and picture-perfect tan, step out of a limo looking miserable. Poor Neal, Maddie looked intently at Cornelious' sour expression. Though she was close with Pilot and Carly, she had to admit Cornelious Gibbz was her best friend. Therefore, it was clear from the look on his face that his father had been explaining that, as the sole heir to the family fortune and as the Governor's son, he will be expected to be perfect in every area and, most likely, make better friends.

"Let's go see why he's so upset," Carly whispered as she and Pilot made their way to Cornelious, through the gathering crowd of anxious onlookers.

Sighing, Maddie pushed her way past her curious peers to join her pals.

"Yes, I know…make new friends, sir. I got it," Cornelious rolled his eyes.

"Very well, good day then," satisfied, Jeremiah pulled the door shut, and the limo peeled away.

Looking up, Cornelious saw three familiar faces coming toward him---or at least trying. Carly---mentally practicing for her big tryout, Pilot---looking a little nervous, and Maddie--- her usual fearless self. Cornelious chuckled and pushed past the slowly evaporating crowd. "Hey guys---" but he was interrupted by the bell. "Well, I guess high school is ready for us," Cornelious stated after the gang had finally met up with each other.

"Nah, it just thinks it is," smiled Maddie as the gang turned and faced the unknown.

2

"GGGGIIIIBBBZZZ!!!!"

Cornelious knew Eric Henry was heading his way, even before glancing up from his locker to see a blonde kid donning a blue polo and khakis walking toward him. Cornelious could only laugh at their vast differences: Eric desperately wanted to live off of the Henry fortune, and have a comfortable life (never having to work a day), whereas Cornelious preferred not to be a Gibbz, for which he was already known.

"Gibbz! My main man! How was preseason? I hope Cap doesn't keep me on Freshmen forever since I missed preseason completely. What have you been up to all summer?

Let me tell you, Greece is beautiful, so is Milan...."

Cornelious unpacked his bookbag, as Eric rambled on and waited for the point to Eric's constant change in conversation. "So...you nervous for the new year? I mean, it's all going to be different now that we're in high school, ya know?"

"I guess it'll be a little different...but we pretty much know everyone already, and we both made the football team, right?"

"Oh yeah...right. You get Varsity letters, and I get Freshmen privileges, which are pretty nil..."

"Maybe after Cap sees your skills you'll get moved up. Anyway, what's your first period?"

"Yeah sure... I'm definitely stuck with the Freshmen scrubs. And I got Basic Math, which I know you are not in," Eric tittered as he marveled at Cornelious' ability to have such natural talent for sports, while also getting high grades in school. Eric used to think he just cheated off of Maddie Petrozza, but he recently began to think otherwise.

"Yeah, sorry. I have Honors English with Ms. Moskow."

"Oh, rough. I heard that chick is nuts," Eric laughed. "Speaking of chicks, have you seen Michelle Walton? Talk about hot!"

"Dude. I've seen her every year, since Kindergarten."

"I know that! But let's just say she grew," Eric laughed again as he wiggled his trimmed, yes trimmed, eyebrows.

"I agree with Eric," laughed a brawny boy with a newly-shaped black mohawk, already sporting a T-shirt that read Asbury High Varsity.

"Hey Jason, I guess you're ready for practice." Cornelious high-fived his father-approving friend, and motioned towards Jason's hair, "What's with the new look?"

"Oh, this baby? I'm just trying to create some cred...for football. And the ladies seem to like it, I may add." Turning from the conversation to face some girls passing by, Jason Scott dragged his hand across the top of his mohawk. Satisfied, he returned to the group. "Anyway, with us being on Varsity...sorry Eric...I thought this would be a good way to show some upperclassmen I'm not messing around."

Cornelious appraised his friend's outfit and had to agree. Jason definitely looked intimidating and much older than a freshman. Cornelious also figured that his idea to recreate his image had come from his father, the notorious TJ Scott.

Before TJ settled down, he was an All-American football star at Asbury High. After a successful six years and two rings in the NFL, a back injury sidelined TJ for good. Lucky for him, at the time he had recently married an NFL cheerleader and accumulated quite a few famous contacts. With the money he had saved and invested, he constructed The Luxurious Lady condominiums---located between the boardwalk and Split Park (split because it was located on the invisible East-West Asbury borderline, and enjoyed by both East and West Asburyans), with an incredible view of the ocean. Throughout the years, any rumor of a celebrity in Asbury brought binoculars and crazed-fans outside the gates of The Luxurious Lady. The Luxurious Lady, in and of itself, drew tourists and newcomers each year, as they gathered outside the gates to gawk at its architectural uniqueness. Not only is every inch of the building painted in bright pink, but the building itself actually resembles a lady. With porches jutting out of each rounded side of the building, baby blue window dressings on the second floor only (out of six floors), two attic windows that constantly glow like eyes, and a curving roof that flowed out onto each ledge like hair, the Luxurious Lady was a piece of art. But ever since Maddie commented on its similarity to a crushed angry crab, Cornelious never saw it the same way.

"Whatever, man. Freshmen are supposed to be on the Freshmen team, hence the name. You two are just athletic freaks," Eric declared.

While Eric and Jason rambled on, Cornelious suddenly wished Pilot was here to talk about something other than football. He'd probably question why the high school had to be so huge, and make some joke about rewiring the computers to enlist an architectural company to downgrade the school's size. At least Cornelious could stand Pilot's crazy rambling.

"Anyway, back to our earlier discussion. If you want to talk about hotness, let's not forget Carly Cosentino. Am I right?" Jason nudged Eric, who tittered in agreement.

"Uh, Jason, remember she's like my sister, and I don't exactly think you're her type." It was always awkward when Jason or any of his other friends (or father-approving, as Cornelious liked to call them), would bring up his best friends.

"If by 'I'm not her type' you are referring to that computer geek Conductor---"

"His name's Pilot." Cornelious turned to face Eric and was genuinely shocked that Eric had actually stood up to Jason, for once. "And besides, Neal and him are tight...remember?"

"Whatever, Pilot's got nothing on me." Jason glared at Eric, who simply checked his watch as if the time was of dire importance.

The bell rang before Cornelius could reply, and Eric and Jason darted off, leaving Cornelious fumbling at his locker.

****

"Cornelious Jeremiah Gibbz?" Ms. Moskow looked up from the attendance sheet, as if utterly surprised that someone was absent or tardy, even though there was no clock in the classroom to judge time. "Cornelious Jeremiah Gibbz?"

"He'll be here, I mean he's here. In the school. But just not here. Yet," Maddie answered, praying he would get here soon, because this lady looked a little, well...distant.

"Ah, what a conundrum, he is here, but yet he is not. Now, that is something to mull over," Ms. Moskow stated as if this was an unforeseen problem only she could resolve. Just as she was about to state something more confusing, Cornelius entered the classroom, looking a little confused himself.

"You must be...Cornelious Jeremiah Gibbz?" Ms. Moskow questioned. Cornelious could now see why she was so 'discussed' by fellow students. Ms. Moskow looked to be in her mid-twenties and was wearing glasses four sizes too big, as well as a poncho, and rainbow socks (in crocs), over her jeans. Her strawberry blonde hair couldn't be tamed, and exploded from underneath the bedazzled rag that she used as a headband.

"Umm, yes, I am. You can just call me Cornelious…or Neal."

"Well, Cornelious or Neal it is then. Nice to meet you." She motioned over to the empty desks and smiled.

Cornelious was happy to find that she carried on without reprimanding him for his lateness. Sliding into a seat beside Maddie, he hurriedly explained how he had completely passed the second floor, ending up on the third floor. Only after a junior had advised him to find the door on the second floor that appears homemade, did he figure out which door to enter. In fact, the whole room appeared 'homey'. Instead of the usual linoleum flooring, Ms. Moskow carpeted the floor in dark purple and covered the walls in quotes from both the famous and the anonymous. Ms. Moskow had apparently exchanged her classic metal teacher's desk and chair, with a hand-carved wooden desk and cushioned stool, with a long orange lamp as her only source of light. Evidently, the desks were the only things school-mandated---but were arranged in a U-shape, allowing plenty of floor space for the students to sit during future group discussions. No one forgot their time spent in this classroom.

"I told you this school is huge," Maddie whispered.

"Madeline Isabella Lydia Natalie Cecilia Petrozza?" inquired Ms. Moskow.

14

Maddie blushed as there were several snickers to her outrageously long name and answered, "Here."

Ms. Moskow nodded and finished up reading the remaining names. "Hello, class. I am sure what with the time-space continuum and parallel universes we have already met," began Ms. Moskow at which Cornelious and Maddie exchanged looks. "But I want to inform you all that in my class-home we are a family, and I would like to be treated in the same way that would you treat your mother."

Several guys made inappropriate, yet funny and expected comments at this statement, but Ms. Moskow continued on. "Our first assignment is to read 'Slaughterhouse 5', which we will discuss at length on Monday."

"Wait a minute. Today is Thursday," Alexis Johnson spoke up.

"Ah, we are blessed to have someone in here who has mastered the fine art of reading calendars," Ms. Moskow smiled.

At Ms. Moskow's comment Maddie couldn't contain her laughter, which sparked somewhat of a laughing phenomenon as many of her classmates joined in as well. Maddie realized she was actually excited to be in school. For as long as she could remember not only had she been competing against the perfectly-curly-redheaded Alexis Johnson for valedictorian of the class, but she had always wanted to gag over her suck-upy ways.

"Obviously, I know what you're insinuating," Alexis managed to retort, "but what I'm saying is this means we only have four days to read a book!"

"But don't you mean four nights, for today has already been established." Ms. Moskow began handing out books, "This book may be an easy read and is rather short in length, but it contains a complex plot and many issues, which I believe is a wonderful way to start off your high school careers. And now I believe our time today is finished, have a fantastic day!" And just like that, the bell rang.

****

By the time fifth period arrived Maddie was starving. Because she had to take Eddie's crazy bus, she had skipped breakfast and was now reaping the consequences.

"Mads! Over here!"

With her tray in hand containing God knows what, Maddie maneuvered her way over to where Carly and Cornelious were sitting in the left corner, near a sign that had once read "ASBURY HIGH WELCOMES NEW STUDENTS," but had evidently been changed to "ASBURY HIGH WELCOMES NUDES," after a few letters were crossed off.

"Where's Pilot?" Maddie questioned, eyeing the sign.

"Huh? Oh no! I lost him! How could I do that?!" Carly looked on the brink of tears, that is until she looked up and saw an explosion of red hair coming their way.

"I'm right here. Cool your jets. You know, you're not my mother, I can look after myself." Pilot replied but was obviously relieved they had saved him a spot in the overcrowded and bustling cafeteria.

16

"'Ow haf ur day bin?" Cornelious asked, mouth full of manwich sloppy joe.

"What? Oh that's just gross," Carly looked at Cornelious and then Pilot, who had begun to eat his manwich as well.

"What?" both boys asked in confusion.

Obviously, neither of them had ever been a teenage girl where eating disgustingly was as bad as breaking a commandment, or sometimes worse.

"Anyway...Maddie guess what?" Carly shifted around to face Maddie, and ignore the boys.

"What?" Maddie asked, knowing she was about to hear some juicy gossip whether she wanted to or not, because, for some reason, Carly always knew everything.

"I saw Trent and Mia, totally flirting it up."

"HA-HA, yeah sure. My brother the dirtball, and your sister the beauty queen," Maddie laughed at the thought.

"No seriously. I mean, all summer she would drive over to your dad's car shop to get her convertible 'tweaked.' It makes sense that she was just looking for an excuse to see him." Carly smiled, content with the satisfaction of her logic. And Maddie had to admit it sounded pretty logical.

"I have to admit it sounds pretty logical."

"I know, right? Plus, your brother's hot."

This statement took Maddie by surprise, causing her to spit out some milk.

"WHAT?" Both Maddie and Pilot asked.

"What? It's true. I mean he works outside on cars, which means he's tan and muscular."

"But he has no brains, no offense Maddie," Pilot sounded a little edgy, and no longer showed interest in his manwich.

"No, I agree," Maddie agreed wholeheartedly.

"Well, I don't care. He IS hot, and that's that," Carly said, and with that, she dug into her dry tuna salad.

****

The rest of the classes flew by rather quickly as far as first day courses go. Fortuitously for the gang, they had managed to get ninth (last) period study hall in the new library. With the newest computers lining the back walls, and a flat screen in each corner, the library was clearly the optimum place for study hall or hanging out if one has senioritis. Walking past the front desk, one must first pass through two detectors (which pick up traces of metal and stolen library property). An array of new magazines waiting to be opened sat by the librarian's desk and Pilot had his eye on Wired Weekly, a local electronics magazine. In order to acquire this magazine, Pilot would have to pass the librarian's desk and pluck up the courage to ask Cunningham for a copy.

The librarian, Mrs. Cunningham, was infamously known for her avid love of animals and ability to correctly detect a lie. Unfortunately for Maddie, Cunningham was also known for scoping out the students at the top of their class and then recruiting them to her book club. Book lovers without top marks need not sign up for the club, for their opinions were often taunted by Cunningham. However, even worse was her hatred for those not in her book club. Which, in essence, made no sense because much more would join if not for her refusal to admit students who didn't fit her standards.

"Yo, Pi, did you manage to get us all here?" Cornelious questioned knowing his friend's magical touch with computers.

"I thought it'd be nice if we managed to get last period together to talk about our day, ya know?" Pilot answered nonchalantly, as he broke out his own laptop and looked longingly at the magazine stacks.

"How thoughtful," Carly smiled at Pilot, who blushed and continued hacking into whatever database he found interesting.

"Yeah, but where's Maddie?" Cornelious asked scanning the room. He didn't have to look long, for he saw Maddie standing in the stacks talking to one of the hottest girls he had ever seen.

"She's talking to Rachel Maer." Carly said without even turning to see her friend, as her mind was focusing on far more important matters such as cheerleading tryouts, which were the next day.

"Who?" Pilot and Cornelious questioned.

"Don't you guys know any of the A-List people around here?" Carly threw her hands up in emphasis.

"No."

"Not really."

Looking her over, it was easy to see why she was an A-Lister: Her long chestnut hair traveled down her mid-back without a strand falling out of place. Obviously, Rachel spent some serious time sunbathing on the beach, and her lips were painted a dark shade of red that guys enjoyed and girls emulated.

Obviously frustrated at having to explain, "Well, that's Rachel Maer. Her father's in real estate and her mother, well she doesn't do much---

"Besides her husband," joked Pilot and Cornelious laughed in agreement.

"You two... seriously. I thought you were more mature."

"We're only freshmen."

"Yeah, give us some time."

"Anyway," Carly glared at the boys, stopping their laughter in its tracks. "Rachel's a senior who plays soccer and happens to be Maddie's big sister this season."

"Big sister? I think she has enough siblings as it is," Cornelious quipped, mentally counting Maddie's five siblings.

"Clearly I'm not speaking literally. The female sports in Asbury have this big-little sister program so the incoming players feel welcome," Carly explained.

"Nice, maybe she'll introduce us," Cornelious said more to himself than to the other two, as Maddie and Rachel finished their chat.

"Thanks. I was just making sure," Maddie said as she walked over to where the gang was gathered. "So...who's thinking tacos after school?"

"Not me, I have to practice," Carly replied unsmiling, visibly racing through routines in her head, and muttering chants under her breath.

"Oh come on. You know you're in perfect shape,"

muttered Pilot.

"Perfect? PERFECT?! Have you ever seen me land a triple back tuck jump?! No! Because I haven't!" Carly stormed out before the bell, officially ending their first day at Asbury High.

3

Brady's Tacos and Pancakes may sound like a weird combination for a restaurant, but they truly do serve the world's best pancakes and tacos. Even stranger than its name may be its boardwalk location, surrounded by beach stores and seafood restaurants. However, Brady's vast differences from its neighbors help account for its success and extreme popularity. Or maybe their success is attributed to serving the best food in town, with a very charismatic staff. The two Head Chefs, Brandan and Dennis, are arguably the best chefs in the nation. After years of studying at Upper Estates Culinary Academy, one of the most prestigious culinary schools in the country, they chose to settle down in a small town. Fortunately for the folks of Asbury, they picked here.

At first glance, it may be easy to doubt the two celebrated chefs. Both men were tall, standing identically at six foot three, and with their burly build, it was easier to imagine them arm-wrestling or building houses than it was to picture them preparing a Consommé. And, with their light brown hair (streaked with blonde due to consistent sun exposure), and boyish good looks, some shoobies thought they were being 'punk'd' when introduced to the cooks. Nevertheless, Asburyans often discovered that judgment was best passed after discovering all the facts for oneself.

Walking from Asbury High to Brady's was basically a pilgrimage for students all over Asbury. The best thing about Asbury High, at least to the students, is that situated behind the school is the boardwalk and the beach. Thus, to get to Brady's one has to walk up the ramp, and travel down the boardwalk for less than two minutes. Once on the boardwalk, the restaurant is anything but inconspicuous, as it has a giant pancake man battling a giant taco man on the roof. The sign itself constantly changes color and can be seen from miles away. Some even propose NASA astronauts view it from space.

Pilot, Maddie, and Cornelious walked through the door and crossed the white and black tiled floor. Since Brady's is usually packed after school, they had to maneuver past the growing crowd to sit in their usual booth near the kitchen and await their favorite waitress. After a hectic day in a new school, where promise and anxiety run high, the trio was ravenous.

"Hey kids! I saved your booth for you, so tell me...how was high school?" asked a beautiful waitress in her early thirties.

"It was a blast! Pilot even got a girlfriend!" Maddie smiled, provoking Cornelious to join in on the fun.

"Yeah, I'm telling you it was love at first sight!"

"AWWWWW! My baby!" the lovely red-headed waitress boomed.

"Mom! They're only kidding!" Pilot responded as he laid his head down on the tabletop, ears singeing red with embarrassment. Though it was awesome having his mom work at Brady's to give them discounted food whenever they wanted, it was humiliating when she carried on as if he was a baby. Especially with half of Asbury High within earshot.

"Oh, well. Sorry if I was excited," Pilot's mother exhaled. "Anyway, the usual?" Without waiting for a reply, Ms. Owens headed back into the kitchen and pulled out six of the most delicious trays ever created---all filled with Brady House Original Beef Tacos. At first glance, a Brady House Original Beef Taco appears to be a mistake and a gross one at that. For this taco is unlike any other. The Original Beef Taco consists of deliciously homemade beef with special sauce, doused in Dennis and Brandan's self-created cheese mix, in a hard taco---on the inside. This delectable gooey gourmet is actually wrapped inside of a plain pancake---when locals order it they just ask for the taco pancake. The non-locals usually need a lot of convincing before daring to taste.

However, just one bite ensures a lifetime addiction to the treat, and yes it's guaranteed on the menu.

"Yes, that'd be delicious," Cornelious' mouth was already watering at the sight of such promising food.

"Oh, Neal! How is my favorite East Asbury young gentleman doing on this fine day?"

"Just fine. School was lovely, especially with your role-model son by my side." Cornelious knew how to make a mom proud, especially one who has had to raise a son by herself since the tender age of eighteen.

I don't care what anyone says, Jenna Owens had nothing to be ashamed of, and especially not Pilot, Maddie thought. After her parents disowned her, she was forced to raise Pilot on her own. As luck would have it, the Petrozza family had been childhood friends with the Owens' and when they announced they were moving to Asbury, Jenna had been the one who alerted the Petrozza's of an open house next door to her own. Maddie smiled as she considered life's mysterious ways.

As they ate their precious taco pancakes they discussed the upcoming weekend activities.

"Well I have practice tomorrow and a game Saturday," Cornelious said as he downed his Oreo milkshake. "Since tryouts were in the summer and all."

Maddie sighed, "Yeah, pretty much the same, except our first game is tomorrow."

"Jeez, you two are so busy. You really know how to make a guy sound like a loser. I guess I'll have to help my mom here tomorrow and bus."

"You know…you could join tech club----" Cornelious started.

"Ha! Yeah right. I taught myself how to do what they're learning now when I was in, let's see…FOURTH GRADE!" Pilot smirked as he finished off his taco. Then he reflected on his personal interests and added, "Besides half of what I do is…uh…'frowned upon' by the law, so I don't know how long it'd keep my interest."

Maddie looked at a sullen Pilot, and added, "Well, if Carly makes the squad---which we know she will--- we could come in here after our practices, eat a little, then catch a film. You know, what with all the free tickets you managed to get."

Pilot smiled and their weekend plans were decided.

****

Maddie stayed at Brady's with Pilot to bum a ride home from Ms. Owens, who was more than happy for some extra girl-talk. She probably wished Carly was here to give her some actual girl-talk, Maddie thought. I'm pretty much useless in that area. I only smile and say 'yeah, I know, right?'

"And Betty Michaels---nicest old lady in West Asbury---insists on dying her hair blue every Friday. I swear there won't be any blue dye left in Asbury."

"Yeah, I know, right?" Maddie smiled.

Still, Ms. Owens always wanted a daughter, in addition to Pilot, and was happy to talk to anyone. Therefore, Maddie felt it was her duty to keep up any conversation that Ms. Owens started.

****

Cornelious decided not to call the limo and opted to take the trolley home to 2234 Red Oak East Asbury: the glorious home of a family richer than the Queen herself---or so deemed by magazines and newspapers. In order to get to the Gibbz mansion, Cornelious had to walk to the main gate and state his name, twice. Then after walking up a gravel driveway, surrounded by weeping willows and pines (for six minutes), Cornelious had to stop again at the second gate and present his credentials. Or in his case, tell Mike he was home. After passing through the gate, Cornelious walked around the circular cobblestone driveway, past what Mr. Gibbz dubbed the 'American Trevi Fountain,' and up the eight concrete steps to their brick-layered mansion. Inside, the style was modern art deco, and appeared to be ripped out of Millionaire's Magazine.

Coming home was definitely Cornelious' least favorite part of the day. In as much as Jeremiah Gibbz was overbearing, Nancy Gibbz was juvenile. Though she never lifted her voice at her son, she needed as much attention and maintenance as the Golden Gate Bridge. With her long, poker straight black hair always down to her hips, azure eyes, and pale skin that never seemed to tan (even when vacationing in the Caribbean for weeks), Nancy seemed doll-like.

"Oh, honey we were worried about you!" Cornelious heard his mother coo. Taken back by his mother's sound of alarm, Cornelious was unable to reply. That is until he peered into the dining room to his left, and realized it was not he who his mother was referring to, but rather their fat cat Howie. Cornelious was not often surprised by his mother, for she was rather predictable in her actions. So when Cornelious saw his mother holding herself and on the verge of tears, watching the Help climbing up on chairs on top of one another trying fruitlessly to drag the obese cat down from the lavish china cabinet, Cornelious was anything but shocked.

"Hey mom," Cornelious called making his way up the marble stairwell to his room, knowing his greeting would go unnoticed.

"Cornelious Jeremiah, please make your way to the library. Your father wishes to speak with you," came a feminine voice over the PA System. Cornelious went to the third floor and pushed open the two oak doors revealing a library the size of a basketball court---which is precisely why it's Maddie's favorite room in the house, Cornelious pondered.

"You know that voice would be sexy, if it wasn't a robot," Cornelious joked.

"Always joking, never serious," rang the voice of his father, who was sitting in his favorite plush armchair situated behind his mahogany desk and stacks of classified papers, reading a manual of some sort. "How was school?"

"Fun, actually. Well, some classes. Madd---er, uh Eric Henry is in three of my classes. And I saw Jason Scott a few times throughout the day, sir." Cornelious was about to tell his father which classes he had with Maddie, Pilot and Carly, but knew it would be grounds for another lecture. Well, not Carly, after all, she is a fellow East Sider.

"You actually seem to be mingling with the right people. I am surprised...but nevertheless impressed."

"Can I go to bed now? I have some homework I need to finish before tomorrow's practice, sir."

"Very well, good night. You are dismissed."

Thank God, thought Cornelious, that actually wasn't too bad. Climbing up one more set of stairs he came to the end of a hallway where an old bookcase stood and pulled out his favorite book: 'Harry Potter and the Deathly Hallows.' Stepping back, the bookcase slid aside and Cornelious made his way up a set of stairs into his single place of solitary---his bedroom. Many considered Cornelious lucky, after all, he is the sole heir to billions of dollars--which made his bedroom rather impressive. Cornelious had chosen the highest room in the house to serve as his living quarters (as he liked to refer to it). Possessing almost every advance in technology had made him quite the popular kid over the years. Yes, he had a jacuzzi bathtub in his personal bathroom, and a walk-in closet to boot, but he usually ignored all the 'toys' his dad bought him and crashed on his bed with his mac.

As far as wealth went, the further east one lived signified the more money one made, which is precisely why Jeremiah Gibbz had built their mansion at the easternmost point in Asbury. From their mansion, one could view the beautiful shoreline and the high school right behind it, or the various restaurants and stores in the downtown section of East Asbury. However, if one was to shift their attention to West Asbury, they would see the apartments, fire station, library, junkyard, and even the Auto Shop in the distance. Cornelious tended to look over to the auto shop where Pilot and Maddie lived, and dream he was their neighbor too. Pilot and Maddie had told him he was ridiculous to hate his riches and should feel lucky he was so fortunate. But as he crossed over to the large bay window that looked over most of Asbury, he wished he could be anywhere but here.

****

"MADDIE! YOU DID NOT CALL OR INFORM ME OTHERWISE WHERE YOU WERE!"

Uh-oh, Maddie thought, she is pissed. "Mom, I'm sorry, it's just--

"NO EXCUSES! YOU ARE GROUNDED!" Natalie Petrozza bellowed as she stood in the kitchen, wringing the kitchen towel as if it were to blame for her daughter's tardiness. Maddie eyed the towel and was glad her mother was preoccupied twisting the towel, rather than her neck.

"Mom… Come on! You're being unreasonable. I was at Brady's with Ms. Owens."

Taking a deep breath, Mrs. Petrozza conceded, "Well, you could've been kidnapped for all I know," Maddie was glad that her mother had at least stopped yelling.

"I will definitely call you next time, maybe if Trent would give me a ride home----

"Oh, no! Don't bring...me...into this! It's not my fault....you...missed curfew," Trent called, out of breath from the next room, where he and Alec were visibly wrestling over the remote. After a couple of yelps, crashes, and some other indistinguishable sounds were heard, Maddie continued, "But I don't see why he can't just take me to school! I mean, Mia takes Carly!"

"Well, Mia's nicer than me. Plus, I told you, you can always pay me," laughed Trent as he tore the remote away from his younger brother. Alec, knowing it was a lost cause, resigned back to his room, leaving Trent bursting with laughter.

"Plus honey, he has football and you have soccer. And what with your social schedule and your friends, there really isn't time."

Maddie gave up, satisfied her mom had forgotten her anger and said "Okay, you're right mom. Hey, where's dad?"

"He's picking up Daniel and Shannon…they had a play date with the Sobrinski children."

"Oh…. How was work?"

"Tiring. Those Henrys may pay well, but their house is always a mess!"

"What else would you expect? But how'd you get those scratches?" Maddie questioned, suddenly alarmed.

"These? Well… the Gibbz' old fat cat got itself stuck up in their china cabinet, again. So we all had to try to get it down. Oh! What a production that was!" Mrs. Petrozza laughed, and Maddie was suddenly in awe of her beautiful, yet strong mother who had raised six kids on her cleaning job salary, and her husband's car shop. Fellow Asbury citizens commented on her mother's beauty and often remarked how similar Maddie looked to her mother. Maddie herself never saw the resemblance.

"What?"

"Huh?" Maddie blinked, realizing she was staring at her mother and had totally zoned out.

"Maddie, darling, you're sitting there smiling. Oh, did you meet a cute boy today?" Mrs. Petrozza turned to Maddie basically begging her daughter to answer with the desired response.

"Mom...ugh." Maddie wanted to explain that there was no time for a boyfriend (with school, sports, and hanging with the gang) and that there weren't any guys she liked enough. But of course, this wasn't something you'd tell your mom. "I have to go read, good night," Maddie got up to make a quick exit.

"Hey! Don't even think about going to bed without a goodnight kiss," Mrs. Petrozza said extending her arms to her oldest daughter and smothering her with a kiss on the cheek.

"Ew, c'mon mom," Maddie said, backing away from her smiling mom and swiftly climbing up the stairs. Upon entering her room she realized her younger sister Sophia was crying in her bed.

"What's up, Soph?" Maddie asked as she threw her bookbag aside and readied herself for some drama.

"It's Billy! He said he wants to break up!" Sophia explained through sobs.

"Listen, boys drool, girls rule." Maddie crossed over to where her sister was lying, and began to stroke her very curly black hair, just like their mother's.

"That's easy for you to say, you've never had a boyfriend."

Touché, Maddie thought and smirked, "And I've never cried over a boy either."

Still, Maddie crawled into bed and allowed Sophia to sleep in her room. After Maddie was sure her younger sister was comfortable, she stroked Sophia's curls and fell asleep telling her younger sister stories to take away her fourth-grade troubles.

4

"That was the worst!" Maddie exclaimed, as she and Cornelius exited their highly-despised Geometry classroom. "Honestly, there's no need for half of this stuff! Proof? What in God's name is a Proof? This syllabus looks intense."

"Tell me about it. I was ready to gouge my eyes out!"

"Well, at least we have Arts and Crafts next with Miss D."

All Geometry-driven anxiety melted away. "True that. She's definitely my favorite teacher by far."

Maddie smiled in agreement as they walked down a flight of stairs, and past endless dull white walls. The two stopped outside a brightly lit doorway that lit up the hall as if it were a beacon for students to release their stress.

"Welcome, welcome! My lovies!" Miss D called out to her students as they filed into her classroom. Miss D is, what most would deem, a hippie---constantly sporting a loose tie-dye shirt with loose khakis and multi-colored flip-flops. By far, her best trait was the need to bring everyone into her heart. In fact, anyone who has ever met Miss D has walked away smiling. Thus, Miss D wasted no time in explaining to her 'lovies' the necessity of treating every art utensil as a loved one.

Cornelious and Maddie took their seats to the left of the room against the windows, near the giant kiln. Although it was arguably the worst spot in the class, as freshmen they had very little say in seating arrangements. On the plus side, Maddie and Cornelious sat on the far end of the table, away from the shelves that smelled like Donegan's Pawn Shop---or death plus sauerkraut and anchovies.

"Hey guys, I heard we're making lovey-dovey doves today."

Although Miss D's class was already one of their favorites, having Nya Carr in Arts and Crafts with them made the class much more exciting. Although Nya wasn't the brightest student, she sure was the funniest. And, although only 5'10", give the girl a basketball and you were sure to win a championship.

"Man Nya, I didn't see you at all this summer? Where'd you go?"

"Well, Cornelious, I actually visited my mother's family in Mali for a month and a half. It was awesome! I always knew we were of Dogon heritage, but you should've seen the masks we had to wear and the dances we performed each night." Nya started to rise from her seat to dance, but sat back down when Miss D broke up the chattering group by giving directions to their project: "Make a lovey-dovey dove, with extra love."

"Will we be graded on the love?" Nya questioned.

"Good question...I'll be right back, I'm going to go try to discover the answer," Miss D replied as she gracefully left the front of the room and walked to the back near the sinks. She quietly entered the dark room, an entirely pitch-black room supposedly used for photographic purposes, and meditated. With Miss D's exit, the class became a study hall for the academic-inclined and a rumor mill for all the rest.

"Aww man. This class is easy and all, but if we have to do girl-projects everyday, I'm gonna die," Cornelious groaned.

"And what exactly do you mean by 'girl-projects'?" Nya jokingly inquired.

"You know what I mean. Maddie explain it to Nya."

"I'll be right back...I have to go ask Rachel about soccer practice. Liz said we find out who's starting today." Maddie nervously rolled her eyes and walked over to where the upperclassmen were currently playing with glueguns or gossiping, or both.

Until Maddie had mentioned it, Cornelious hadn't realized there were upperclassmen in the class, let alone ultra-hottie Rachel Maer. After looking at her, he couldn't believe he had missed her. With her hair hanging loosely over her shoulders, she smiled as she talked, showing off her perfect set of teeth. Cornelious didn't even realize Maddie had returned, and was apparently speaking to him, until she was snapping her fingers in his line of vision.

"What?"

"I was saying that Kurt Vonnegut---hey!"

"Sorry, I just dozed off," Cornelious lied, hoping he wasn't being too obvious.

"You're a terrible liar... I know exactly what you were doing," Maddie whispered so Nya wouldn't overhear, "you have a thing for Rachel Maer."

"What? No I don't!"

"Admit it, I won't tell. Who would I tell anyway?" Maddie wondered.

"Okay, okay. But look, she's an athlete so you know she has a great bod, plus I heard she's pretty smart," Cornelious listed.

"Yeah, pretty much number one in her year." Maddie smiled, as she traced an intricately woven wicker basket onto paper, in which to house the lovey-dovey-dove.

"What?" Cornelious wanted to know what was so funny.

"It's cute. You're so defensive about a crush. Look, you're blushing."

"Shut up!"

****

Pilot had somehow managed to get his schedule switched so he now had fourth-period Economics with Maddie and Cornelious, as well as seventh-period Gym. And by somehow managing to get his schedule switched, he hacked into the school's security and made his perfect schedule---which included four classes with Maddie and Cornelious and seven with Carly. Although happy to have Pilot in their classes, they also urged him to try to make some more friends.

"I have plenty of friends," Pilot whispered in response. "There is Karuto, Kalif, Pierre, Ping-Tau…"

"Online friends from foreign countries whom you have never met in person do NOT count," Maddie explained, holding up a finger in emphasis.

"They do if we have similar interests and chat all the time," Pilot challenged.

"That's just weird, dude. Seriously." Cornelious quipped, but then stopped when he saw Mr. Chase strut into the gymnasium, imposing and in control.

"Since today is only your second day of school, I can't permit you to perform physical activities. Thus, you will listen as I speak to the seriousness of physical activity and how I can ruin your precious GPAs if you choose not to partake in our endeavors."

Which is when Pilot made the mistake of laughing.

"What, in my mama's sweet name, do you find so amusing, BOY?" A balding Mr. Chase now stood head to head with Pilot, and was literally spitting into his face. In fact, Mr. Chase's spit is so powerful (and plentiful), that it's believed his spit alone carved out Mt. Rushmore.

"Well…ummm," Pilot glanced over at Maddie and Cornelious, who were slowly backing away, though the smiles on their faces were evident.

"That's what I thought. Now the school prohibits strenuous physical activity, but they do allow punishment for smart-alecs like you! So drop down and give me fifty. NOW!"

"Way to go, Chase, he needs discipline," Jason Scott laughed and high-fived Eric, as JB chuckled from the corner.

"This class looks promising," Pilot groaned as he threw himself onto the floor, and began his punishment.

"I meant REAL push-ups! Not lazy ones! That just doubles your total, now give me one hundred!" spat Mr. Chase.

Pilot wiped the spit off his face, and silently swore under his breath.

****

"I still can't believe he made you do one hundred push-ups! Does he know how degrading that is?!" Carly fumed. "After school, I'm going to walk right in there and give him a piece of my mind!"

"No, you're not. You can't. You have cheerleading tryouts...oh crap." Maddie said as she looked up to see Eric Henry making his way across the library, to their table. A smile appeared on his face as he slowly handed Maddie a yellow slip.

"You have a guidance pass, Madeline."

"Oh really, that's what this is? Thanks for helping me read. Maybe one day you can teach me so I can read myself," Maddie said.

"It would be my pleasure," smiled Eric bowing to Maddie.

Ignoring his antics, she stormed out of the library.

"She really hates your guts," Cornelious laughed.

"And she has every right to after you almost got her expelled last year!" Carly retorted and turned away from the conversation by opening her giant history book.

"Hey, it wasn't me, for the tenth time. I wasn't the one who told Vice Principal Coste, now Principal of Asbury High I might add---

"I think we all have realized that," Pilot asserted, and then left to get a book from the shelves, or was at least trying to make himself look busy, too.

"Anyway, I told Coste that Alexis helped me cheat, not Maddie. And in the end my dad covered it up anyway, so what?"

"You really have a nice set of ethics there," Carly stated. Sighing, Eric left to go back to his guidance aid duties. "And he probably made Alexis help him," Carly added when she was sure Eric had left.

"You guys should give him a chance. He's really not a bad guy. Just comes from a family with no, er, ethics."

"Neal, honestly he may be the nicest guy on Earth, but as long as Maddie doesn't like him, neither do I. That may sound mean, but he almost screwed her over and then got his father to cover it up. How much could he really change?"

Cornelious was about to respond, when he realized Rachel had entered the library and he completely forgot about the conversation. And Carly forgot the conversation as well, when she noticed Cornelious 'noticing' Rachel.

"So you have a thing for Ms. Perfect, eh?"

"What? Did Mad--"

"Nope, but it sure is obvious," laughed Carly, satisfied that once again she was correct.

"Well, don't tell Pilot. I'll get enough of it from you and Maddie ragging on me all the time."

"Don't tell Pilot what?" Pilot asked as he returned to the table, carrying a magazine on the newest virus, about which papers were warning everyone. Clearly, Pilot was proud that he had found the courage to grab a magazine. But when Cornelious looked over at the stand, he saw Mrs. Cunningham was absent, so basically all of the magazines were in use. "If it's about this virus, then no worries. After all, this is really just a load of crap. Especially if you have a laptop with---"

"Okay, okay I'll tell you," Cornelious surrendered. "It's just that...I...uh. Well, you know…"

"Pilot, Cornelious is seriously crushing on Ms. Rachel over there," pointed Carly, rather disapprovingly. "If you ask me, she's rather superficial."

"You don't even know her!" Cornelious was quick to answer.

"And you do?" Carly countered, but let it drop when she saw Pilot motion for her to cut it out, for Cornelious was looking royally pissed. "Well, what I meant to say is you should meet her, and I can introduce you now if you'd like," Carly smirked and rose from her seat.

Luckily, Cornelious was faster and dragged her down

saying, "No, no. I'll just introduce myself later." Or have Maddie put in a good word, he thought, and quickly turned away after realizing Rachel was looking at him.

5

After being knocked over, knocked out, and quite frankly knocked around, Cornelious was wondering why he had ever signed up for football in the first place. But then he remembered when they scrimmaged and he played with the Varsity---the glory. He wasn't just good at football, he was amazing. Which was exactly what the coach was thinking when he asked Cornelious how he felt about the team.

"Well, I don't know much about the competition, but I think we have a chance to win it all Coach," Cornelious replied. It was easy for Cornelious to talk to adults, for his parents had him mastering this art before they had him walking.

"Well said, Gibbzy boy! NOW HIT THE SHOWERS!!" Coach Cap bellowed to everyone. Yes, Coach Cap was intense, but it was necessary when dealing with boys ranging in age from 14 to 18. During competition, his yelling would get so loud that residents would complain about his noise level---from across town in Caldwell Courts. Truth be told, Cornelious actually did believe he had heard Cap's bellow from Carly's home in Caldwell Courts before. The only way to keep Cap quiet was to win a championship or to put on an '8 Man Marathon.' But, seeing as Japanese Anime Series marathons from the sixties are hard to come by in Asbury, Cap had to settle for championships.

"Dude, wanna head to Brady's?"

"I'm gonna wait for Mads, I'll see ya there."

"Okay, whatever. I'm not heart-broken," Jason wiped away a fake tear and staggered into the locker room.

Cornelious glanced at his watch and was surprised to see practice had ended early. After the shower, he decided he would watch Maddie's practice. After all, he may see Rachel too.

****

"GGGOOOAAALLLL!" came the cry of the very enthusiastic soccer coach at Asbury. Coach Pez was known to be an avid soccer lover, who never took bribes nor allowed special treatment, much to many East-sider's dismay. This season's cause for excitement was a freshman standout, whose skills were unmatched and appeared unstoppable. Fearless is the word, Pez thought as he called the practice to an end.

"Great job, girls. I'll post the Varsity starters for the Saturday game on the school website tonight." Coach Pez was about to turn around when he noticed his number one freshman, and possibly overall player was lingering on the field.

"Coach, can I have a minute of your time?" she asked.

"Why of course, Maddie, what's up?" Coach asked concerned.

"Well. The thing is...our computer is down and I usually use my neighbor's computer, but I have to make sure he's home---or it's humanly impossible to get into his room....so can you tell me if I'm on Varsity? Just so I can tell my parents if it's worth coming."

"Of course you're on Varsity Maddie! You're freakin' unbelievable! In fact, I'm pretty sure you'll play the entire game."

"But doesn't Rachel start over me?"

"She used to, but bear in mind, no spots are definite," winked Pez. "Now I really must go."

Maddie watched her coach drive off and felt a mixture of emotions. First, she was out of her mind with excitement that she had a starting spot on the Varsity! Still, she felt bad that she had taken her 'big sister's' spot.

"But she'll understand, right?" Maddie questioned Cornelious on the trolley to Brady's, where Pilot and Carly were waiting.

"Yeah, well...she should. I mean, if she wants to win then

she should know that you are the better player." Cornelious knew Maddie was a great athlete and hoped that Rachel would realize as much. If Maddie and Rachel were rivals, would he even stand a chance?

"Thanks," Maddie smiled as they hopped off the trolley and they made their way into Brady's.

"We're here, don't worry!" Cornelious called.

"Finally, I'm starving. Guess what? I made the squad!" Carly squealed full of delight.

The rest of the night was filled with stories of the difficult, but worthwhile tryouts, as well as the grotesque tables Pilot had to clean---which, in turn, ended in their being shooed out of Brady's for laughing too loud (a regular occurrence for the gang).

After being forced from Brady's, which led to even more jokes, the foursome found their way to the theater and used Pilot's Passes, as they called them, to enjoy four hours of free movies.

While they were walking down the boardwalk, the gang ran into the Peters twins who warned them against seeing the new comedy.

"We thought it was gonna be better than our favorite and absolute classic, 'The Hangover.' But after seeing it, we feel like we have hangovers from the worst cinematic experience of all time," Peetie joked. The Peters twins, Peetie and Jazz, may look alike, but their personalities often clashed, leaving most wondering how they were so close. Peetie, or Jasmine, had long wavy dirty-blonde hair and large brown eyes. She also got along with everyone, and although from West Asbury, she never wore the same outfit twice and always dressed, well presidential. Furthermore, with the recent election, she had just made history by being the first freshman to be elected the President of Student Council of Asbury High School. While Jazz, or Jasper, also had shaggy dirty-blonde hair and large brown eyes, he didn't exactly get along with everyone. In fact, Jazz chose to speak only to those from West Asbury, as he felt the East Asburyans didn't deserve their good fortune. However, Pilot and Maddie both agreed he was a great friend to have and was very talented musically (in fact, he was never seen without a guitar case hanging from his back).

"Aww man, I was really looking forward to it," Pilot griped.

"Whatever, we'll just see something action-packed instead. Thanks for the advice guys. Oh and congrats Peetie, I voted for you!" Maddie said.

"Me too!" Carly squealed.

"I think everyone did… you're too nice of a person not to vote for," Pilot added.

As the twins walked away, the foursome headed into the cinema, proudly presenting their Pilot Passes. When it was just about eleven, they decided it was time to go their separate ways. Maddie, being her usual dorky self, began acting out one of the scenes from the movie. By complete accident, she had managed to knock into a passerby.

"Oh, I'm sorry…oh, wait, never mind," Maddie said as she

saw it was JB.

"Now, not saying sorry, that was mistake number two, girly," JB sneered, brushing himself off. It was amazing to think this guy, who now stood at six foot two and sported a military buzz cut, was only in the ninth grade. Although he had always been the biggest in the class, this summer he had grown up and filled out. But what he grew in muscle, he lacked in brains, which is why Maddie, Carly, Pilot, and Cornelious could never understand how he became the leader of "The Pitbulls"---a gang of self-proclaimed protectors of the West Siders, who have been quoted on their wishes to make the East Siders pay. However, it appeared that JB had decided to stroll the streets alone tonight, leaving his gang at home, which is why Maddie didn't care what she said to him.

"Oh, really what was mistake number one?" Maddie asked fearlessly.

"Bumping into me of course."

"That was pretty obvious," Carly whispered.

"Hey fellas looks like we got some East Asburys, here. Should've known you'd be with your boyfriend, Madeline," JB laughed. Literally stepping out of the shadows, five fellow Pitbulls (ranging from the eighth grade to third-year seniors) appeared and took their places beside JB.

Maddie hated when people confused her and Cornelious as boyfriend-girlfriend. Can't a girl just have guy friends anymore? Maddie looked back a Cornelious, who just shrugged, and began fiddling with his new watch. Maddie rolled her eyes and turned her attention back to the Pitbulls.

"Don't call me Madeline."

"Whatever. Just give us your jewelry and nobody gets hurt," JB announced.

"Oh, so now you're thieves too?" Pilot bravely asked.

"We just want to even out the difference between East As and West As," JB scoffed as the Pitbulls joined in the fun.

"Oh, how clever JB. Did ya think of that one by yourself?" Maddie prodded.

"ENOUGH TALK!" JB proclaimed, angrily taking a step towards Maddie, causing her to step backward.

"Mr. Gibbz?! Have you been harmed?" boomed an officer over a megaphone. The Pitbulls turned to see two squad cars and their various policemen stepping out of them. But before the police could reach them, the 'fearless' Pitbulls ran back to their doghouses.

"My dad bought me a new military-grade wristwatch with a button for emergencies or something," Cornelious casually told the gang, explaining the policeman's sudden arrival.

"What? And you didn't tell me? That technology must be brand new! You have to let me borrow it. Maybe I can make my own prototype…" Pilot rattled on as the gang climbed into the back of the police car.

"Good. Now we'll just take you all home," smiled a kind officer.

6

October was just beginning, and fall sports in Asbury were officially heating up. Everybody knows how you start and end October effects your playoff standings and bragging rights. Therefore, every game in Asbury High was being treated as a championship. The stress put on the players from high-ranking East-siders only added to the general tension and need to succeed. If the East-siders were disappointed where else would the funding come from?

"That game was rough," Maddie concluded as she collapsed onto her bed, looking up at a giant poster of cookies and milk. Her own personal heaven.

"Well, how'd ya do?" Pilot asked, climbing in her window-

--directly opposite his own bedroom window. Maddie was lucky to have the best room in her house, or so she thought. Not only did she have her own bathroom (although smaller than a Norwegian nook), but her room was isolated as the only room on the third floor. Therefore, her friends were always climbing in through her window (thanks to the sturdy overgrown ivy against the side of the house), without anyone knowing---which was great when she was grounded. With bean bags and a large, lumpy mattress, her friends had plenty of space to crash for the night. People who knew Maddie and her avid love of reading wouldn't have been surprised by the plethora of books scattered about, as well as the three bookcases lining the room, stuffed with books in every open space.

"We won and I scored twice. And it was a big conference match." Even though she sensed he didn't really care, nor know anything about soccer.

"That's good, right?" he asked as he sprawled across the end of Maddie's mattress.

Maddie couldn't help but laugh, for only Pilot, a technological wiz, would not know whether scoring multiple times in a soccer match was good.

"Yes, it's good. So whatcha doin' tonight? Maddie asked.

"A whole lot of nothin'," as was the usual reply whenever Maddie and Pilot were just laying around in her room.

"Well, I'm watching the twins tonight if ya wanna---

"Sure, what else is there to do?"

Maddie and Pilot made their way downstairs just as Mr.

and Mrs. Petrozza were leaving. Mrs. Petrozza was trying to stress that 'you mustn't let Shannon eat too much spicy food,' even though everyone knew that was a losing battle. When it came down to spicy chicken and Shannon, Shannon always won. Luckily for Maddie, Pilot lived right next door and was always able to help. While Pilot played with Daniel and Shannon, Maddie was busy making dinner.

"I got it!" Maddie exclaimed when the phone began to ring.

"Hello, Pilot Owens speaking, who is this?"

"Cornelious."

"PILOT! I SAID I GOT IT," Maddie yelled into the phone, "sorry. What's up Neal? Your dad bothering you again? Should I come over and mess with him?"

Cornelious smiled, "No. Nothing, seriously. So, what, you two on a date or something?"

"Actually we've eloped and are now sharing my humble abode," joked Maddie.

"Makes sense, but what about Carly?"

"Oh, we killed her. I can't have any distractions in my marriage."

"True, true," smiled Cornelious, "so...what are you two up to?

"Just babysitting the dweebs and dweebets."

"Sounds fun."

"Loads." Suddenly Sophia burst into the room with Daniel and Shannon flanking her sides, protesting their innocence, as she held up her new dress with paint and hot sauce stains all over it. "Ugh! I'm really sorry, but I have to go. Trouble and dinner and everything is waiting. Did you want something?" Maddie asked.

"No, not really."

"Okay, sorry. You can stop by if you want."

"Nah, I should study."

Maddie chuckled, "Yeah right. See ya Monday."

"See ya." Cornelious suddenly felt very lonely when he hung up the phone, and looked around his vacant room. Being the only child was bad enough, but being an afterthought to everything his parents did, was oftentimes unbearable. He decided to text Carly and see what she was doing, but she wasn't answering her cell. She was probably practicing some cheerleading maneuvers. Realizing there truly was nothing to do, other than homework, Cornelious did what everyone does to past time. He went online, and his heart skipped a beat when he realized he had a message from...RACHEL MAER! Quickly, he opened the dialogue box to see what she had wrote to him.

"Hey. I heard you had the game-winning touchdown. Congrats superstar :)"

Taking a second to think of a response, he nervously typed, "Thanks, but I just caught the ball and ran.... how was soccer?"

"Boring. We won, but coach has me riding the bench!" At this, Cornelious had no clue how to respond. Wasn't it his best friend who had taken her spot?!

"Oh, I'm sorry. I forgot, Maddie Petrozza is like your

what? Girlfriend?"

"No, no. She is definitely not my girlfriend...we just go way back."

"Oh, so you're single?"

Cornelious was wondering if this was a prank, but he couldn't stop himself. "Yup."

"Huh. Well, see you Monday :)."

Cornelious shut his laptop, mulling over the fact he had just gotten two smiley faces from a girl who didn't even know he existed. Or at least that's what he thought about ten minutes ago. Also, this same girl was apparently very pissed at his best friend. Was this a good thing?

7

During the weekend, Asburyans faced something they never before dealt with: a major break-in into one of East Asbury's most prominent families had resulted in a two-thousand-dollar theft. Although this amount wasn't a lot for an East-sider, the town was full of unrest. For everyone knows the first break-in, is never the last.

"This sucks! My mom tried changing the locks four times before she let us out of the house! Mia had to calm her down just so she wouldn't end up locking us inside of the house."

"Lucky you Carly," Cornelious mumbled, "My mom said that she would die if someone harmed the cat! Not the money. Not the car. Not even me! And then my dad said I'm to come right home after practice and no more hanging out with those hooligans. He honestly thinks you guys broke into the Lomlings!"

Maddie turned to view Kirk Lomling and the pity party he was throwing. If I had been ripped off two grand I wouldn't sit around and ask for everyone's sympathy, Maddie thought watching Kirk spew details and statistics of the improbability of a theft occurring in his security-ridden home---scratch that---mansion. She was about to crack a joke over Kirk's mansion-theft, but when she faced her friends she felt the awkward tension beginning to rise. Suddenly, she thought of a bright idea, "Hey guys! I know what we should do!" Maddie exclaimed and motioned for them all to move closer. Seeing as they were in lunch it was hard enough to hear each other. "We should try to solve this ourselves!"

"Great idea! Why didn't I think of it?!" Carly's voice got higher as she spoke. "Four fourteen-year-olds trying to solve a break-in, now that's hilarious. Oh! I do have one question...why?"

"Well, seeing as our schedules are very different after school, this will be an excuse for us to get together, and we could think of it as an adventure. Plus, we did win the murder-mystery night in middle school each year, eh?"

"Oh yeah I forgot, the robber is obviously Mr. Hayfield dressed up as Colonel Mustard."

"Maddie, it sounds fun. But where would we even start?" Pilot asked, while nervously glancing at Carly, afraid to disagree. The table went silent for a few minutes to reflect on this idea.

"I can't believe we're honestly considering this," Carly interjected, effectively breaking the silence.

"Well, we could start at the Lomling's. You know, it was Kirk's family that was robbed. We could try to find their security room and look at the tapes to see if anything is out of place." Cornelious announced out of nowhere.

"Okay. Cool. So let's----" but before Maddie could finish they were interrupted by the bell.

"STUDY HALL!" Maddie boomed shuffling out the door, and into the hall.

****

"I still don't approve," Carly affirmed as she sat down at the table and pushed Maddie's books aside.

"You don't even know the plan yet," Maddie snapped.

"Whatever, it doesn't matter, we're going to get in trouble either way."

"Not if we don't get caught!" Maddie countered.

"SSSHHH! This is study hall!" the librarian rasped.

"Okay, so here's the pla---oh not again!" Maddie complained as they all looked up to see Eric smirking and making his way over to the group.

"I actually have two passes. One for Ms. Carly, and one for Ms. Sunshine," Eric jested as he handed them the passes.

"Why does Ms. Clarke insist on seeing me all the time?"

"Actually it's only been twice," Eric smiled.

"And it's only the second month of school!" Maddie angrily stated, hating that she was letting Eric Henry push her buttons. Sighing, she and Carly got up from the table and made their way across the hall into the main office. Located inside the main office (which was essentially a large glass cube where secretaries and both vice principals toiled away), was the small guidance office. No matter what anyone said, this place was the exact opposite of soothing--- it gave her the chills.

"I'll see Maddie first," Ms. Clarke called out from her rather boxy, yet superbly decorated office.

"How grand!" Maddie uttered as she entered the pretty brunette's office. Though Maddie was plenty pissed at the moment, she couldn't conceal her smile as she passed under the flashing sign over Ms. Clarke's doorway that read: "The Biggest Little City In The World." The sign was rather tacky, Maddie considered, but hey, at least the lady has some sense of style. Especially when compared to last year's female guidance counselor who looked like Abe Lincoln, post-mortem.

"Now, the last time you were here you told me you had five siblings, and you happen to be the second eldest, am I right?"

"Kudos, you remembered me...I mean you really remembered me!" Maddie gushed.

"While sarcasm and joking may get you far out there," Ms. Clarke pointed to the window, "in here I can see it's just a call for help. Now your mother, what's her occupation?"

"She's a cleaning lady," Maddie stated, and proud of it!

"Does she clean East Asbury or West Asbury?"

"East, obviously. I mean seriously, we West-siders clean our own mess."

"How true. Do you see your mother very often?"

"Yep. She only has six clients, and four of them she cleans during weekdays, and the other two weekend nights, but not every week." Maddie realized that Ms. Clarke had the annoying habit of writing down everything Maddie said, without ever taking her penetrating gaze away from Maddie's eyes.

"Do you feel like you spend quality time with her?"

"Yes. Listen I am loved and I am happy, so can I go now?"

"Hmm," sighed Ms. Clarke, "I suppose, but we will meet at another time."

Maddie got up and was out of there quicker than Michael Phelps in the 100-meter fly. She only paused to bid Carly (who was waiting among the small line of chairs outside Ms. Clarke's room) good luck and notify her that they were meeting at Cornelious' after their practices. Maddie threw open the glass door leading from the main office into the hall, only to run right into Rodney Shiffler. Both fell to the ground, and Maddie apologized about one hundred times before Rodney was even back on his feet.

"It's fine, Maddie, really," Rodney said as he brushed himself off and righted his appearance.

"You...you know me?" Maddie asked. She was very confused. Rodney Shiffler was the star quarterback and most likely going to win both Homecoming and Prom King, there was no way he should know her.

"Sure," he winked and gave her a million-dollar smile, "I know all the good-looking girls."

With that said, he walked happily into the guidance office and took a seat. However, Maddie still couldn't shake the feeling that something was up. There's no way he would or could know her. I know I'm not ugly, Maddie mused, but I'm no Miss America! Or even Carly for that matter, Maddie thought as she glanced back to see her stylish friend walking into Ms. Clarke's little room. Carly may have been just beginning to experiment with fashion, but she was as smooth with make-up as Van Gogh was with a brush. Maddie walked back to where she had left the boys and smiled to find Rachel sitting right next to Cornelious, and one of her friends was playing with Pilot's hair.

"Hey guys," Maddie greeted her friends, and pulled up a seat, much to Pilot's obvious relief.

"Well, we should be going…the bell is about to ring and all. Bye boys," Rachel cooed as she and her friend walked out of the library.

"So?" Maddie asked knowingly.

Sometimes Cornelious hated how she just seemed to know everything, but he always told her anyway. "So… she wanted to know if I had plans after this week's football game."

"And?"

"And, I told her no."

"And… come on! This is like pulling teeth! Just give me the details already," Maddie urged.

"Okay, okay! So, we basically agreed to go to Chase Shacklin's party with them."

"Wait, we who?"

"Me and Pilot of course."

Maddie looked from guy to guy wondering how on Earth they could be so stupid. But here they were, smug as ever. So she asked the question they didn't think of, "Who's gonna tell Carly?"

"Why? What's it matter?" Cornelious asked.

"Yeah, she could come too," Pilot added.

"Well, whatever, never mind," boys sure are stupid she reflected, "I told her we're meeting at your house after our practices so see you there," Maddie said right before the bell rang and they went their separate ways.

8

"Mom, is dad home?" Cornelious asked, silently praying he wasn't.

"No, smuckhums. Remember I told you he has business meetings Mondays and Wednesdays now."

"No, you didn't."

"Oh, well. Then I guess I forgot to tell you." Cornelious opened his mouth to say more, but his mother had left the dining room and was calling after Howie. With nothing more to do, Cornelious entered their deluxe kitchen, that would make even Guy Fieri jealous. There was an ice-cream bar along the back wall, and endless cabinets that were filled with spices, foods, and culinary tools, lined the walls. Walking past the marble waterfall island and its bar stools, Cornelious quickly went to the computer screen next to the back sliding doors and typed in Smorz Pop-Tarts. In the blink of an eye, the warm treat popped out from a small vending-like window in the wall---curtesy of the house computer Jeremiah installed upon moving, knowing his wife and his own lack of culinary abilities. Grabbing his deliciously gooey snack, he headed upstairs to quickly straighten his room. Hearing footsteps heading his way a few moments later, he knew it was time to get down to business.

"Okay let's review the facts," Maddie began as she slid beside Cornelious onto his NASA-engineered-mattress, or as she called it, the world's comfiest bed.

"What facts? There aren't any."

"Come on Carly, give her a break." Maddie was actually surprised to hear Pilot interrupt Carly. And to be honest, Carly was quite taken back, and let Maddie continue without further interruption.

"Anyway, the Lomlings were robbed on a Sunday. Only two thousand dollars were stolen which tells us..." Maddie looked at her friends imploringly.

"What? That he--

"Or she." Carly cut off Cornelious, sticking to her feminist roots.

"That the perpetrator," Cornelious stressed, "sucks."

"Oh, I get it. If he was smart he would've made off with a lot more than two grand, because he would've taken the most valuable things," Pilot stated.

"Or she," Carly smiled.

"Okay, we get it, Car," Cornelious stated.

"Exactly, Pilot. Now, I think the thief is young. Possibly a teenager."

"Why would you say that?" Carly asked. "The robber could've just been very, very stupid."

"True, but I have a feeling the robber may be young and agile. You know, able to sneak in and out of the house...but you're right. We can't jump to conclusions."

Carly straightened up a little from leaning on Cornelious' bean bag chair, feeling as if she contributed something valuable. "Now, I propose we find a way to get into the Lomling's security room and see if they missed anything," Maddie stated rising from the bed to face the bay windows, and in turn the Lomling's large mansion.

"Well, how the heck are we going to manage that?" Pilot asked, visually calculating possible ways to break-in.

"I know exactly how," Cornelious smiled and looked at Pilot, who turned to Maddie, who looked back at Cornelious, and then they all looked at Carly.

"What? Why are you all smiling at me?" But then the realization hit her. "Oh, guys, come on. I'm cheering at the game right before."

"And that can give you an excuse for making sure the date is short," Maddie explained.

"Well...uh, he's gross," Carly begged, knowing she had already lost the battle.

"Think of it as undercover work, not a real date."

"But...but...well...okay. But this is the only time. And you ALL owe me, BIG time."

The gang couldn't hold it in anymore, and before they knew it, they were all exploding with laughter. Carly was about to ask Kirk Lomling---her biggest admirer---on a date.

****

"Hey, Kirk! Wait up!" Carly yelled as she followed a lanky boy sporting a lime-green sweater vest, with brown plaid capris down the hallway.

"WH--Oh, uh, hi there pretty lady, what's happening?" Kirk Lomling asked, greasing back his already perfectly gelled and parted black hair.

"Kirk sure does have a way with the ladies," Cornelious whispered as he, Pilot, and Maddie, walked behind them undetected.

"Oh, you're too much. I was just wondering if you had plans for this Friday?" Carly placed her hand on his shoulder, which caused his face to turn from pale-white to blood-red.

"Let me check my palm-pilot," Kirk whipped out his little mechanical device so fast, Carly was sure she had gotten a backlash from it. Several seconds passed as Kirk beeped and clicked his way through his 'busy' schedule.

"Hey! Are they talking about me?" Pilot whispered at the mention of the word pilot.

"No, dummy. He just took out his calendar-thing," Maddie whispered. "Now, shush it!"

"It just so happens that I, myself, am free on this upcoming Friday night," Kirk licked his lips.

Along with every other night, Carly shuddered. "Well, maybe we could watch a movie at your place...?"

"It would be my greatest honor to play host to a lady such as yourself," Kirk said, as he bowed and, taking Carly's wrist, kissed her hand gently, before proceeding backward into his classroom.

Instantaneously, Maddie and Cornelious erupted with laughter.

"EW! Does anybody have sanitizer!" shrieked Carly.

"Did he just kiss her?!" Pilot asked angrily. "I mean, did his lips actually just touch Carly's skin?!"

"Dude, it was just on the hand, and look she ran to the girls' room," Cornelious was still shaking with laughter, as he pushed open the door to the Economics room.

"Sure, it's the hand now. But what will he expect on Friday night?!" Pilot replied as he took his seat right inside the door.

"Students! Please take your new seats. I have organized you according to my best wishes."

"Hey partner, what's shaking?" Eric laughed as he sat down next to Maddie.

"Oh, God. Just when I was starting to enjoy this class."
****

"I think it'd be best if Carly didn't go to the Lomling's," Pilot stated as soon as the gang was all seated at lunch.

"Are you serious? After I let him kiss my hand?" Carly asked incredulously.

"That is precisely the reason."

Cornelious and Maddie silently agreed to let the two

continue bickering until it boiled over. This occurrence had been happening for about three years now, and both Maddie and Cornelious were just waiting for Pilot to ask Carly out, or more likely, vice versa.

"Do you have any plans for this weekend, I mean after you break into the Lomling's."

Maddie laughed, "Not really. Probably going to help my dad at the car shop."

"Cool." Maddie laughed at this, but Cornelious had really meant it. For years, he had been dreaming his dad would change into someone like Mr. Petrozza, who did things with his kids just for fun, and not for photo ops.

"Okay, well then you shouldn't go alone," Pilot suddenly declared.

"Wait a second. I thought you guys were going to be there. Well sneaking in, I mean."

"I am," Maddie said, but then wished she hadn't.

"And where exactly will you two be?" Carly questioned, dropping her fork and glowering at the boys.

"We...er...will...actually...the thing is...crazy story..." Pilot stammered making sure to avoid eye contact.

"SPIT IT OUT!" Carly screamed.

It's amazing no one could hear us, thought Maddie. But I sure am glad, because this is about to get pretty awkward, or nasty, or maybe even both.

"Carly. The thing is... Me and Pilot, or uh, Pilot and I have dates after the game," Cornelious said uncomfortably.

"What? I don't believe you...Pilot?" His name came out as

more of a whisper than a question.

Misinterpreting Carly's question, Pilot suddenly grew angry. "What? You don't think I'm good enough to go on dates?"

"NO! It's just...well...I," Maddie could tell Carly was on the verge of tears. "OH! I just remembered I left my bag in English," Carly got up and ran out of the cafeteria.

"You are SO dumb," Maddie managed to say.

"What? It's not my fault girls think I'm hot," Pilot said. But Maddie realized he had stopped eating his lunch, and an awkward silence had settled over the table.

Four more years of this? Both Maddie and Cornelious thought to themselves.

9

The week passed pretty ordinarily. There were tests, homework, and essays distributed, as should be expected. However, Maddie was just about on the verge of exploding.

"You and Pilot better have the time of your lives tonight," Maddie said to Cornelious as they sat listening to Ms. Moskow.

"Hey, I'm not the bad guy. I agreed to go on this date before we decided to become detectives!" Cornelious challenged. But he knew Maddie was only upset because Pilot and Carly hadn't said a single word to each other in two days. Which was basically two years by high school standards.

"We all agree 'The Sea Wolf' was an extraordinary novel,

69

written by an extraordinary man. But now we must move on, just like the tired worker ants in the dirt below." Ms. Moskow continued, "We will now be reading 'Metamorphosis'. I want you all to really dive into this book and let it devour you."

"Sounds scary," mumbled Cornelious, at which the class laughed in agreement.

"It sounds scary because it is scary. You all are changing all the time, every day. The person you sit next to now may be your friend, only to become your enemy within a couple years. You yourself, may discover your untapped potential and continue to grow throughout life!"

Cornelious looked over at Maddie and thought that they could never be enemies. But then he realized that she was completely buying this crap. Though Cornelious really liked Ms. Moskow, he knew when she was going off on a rampage it was best to zone her out.

"So students, please don't be afraid to come to me with questions about this book or life in general. For I may have some questions that only you can answer. After all, we are all teachers just as we are all learners. Go in peace!"

Ms. Moskow's uncanny ability to know exactly when the bell was going to ring shocked Cornelious every time.

"Were you actually buying that?"

"What? Oh, Ms. Moskow's speech? Well, I thought it was interesting. Unlike Geometry with Mr. McKlien the bore."
****

"Hey, do you think we should get together and work on our stock market project this weekend?" Eric leaned over to ask Maddie, who was apparently not paying attention.

"What? Uh, no. That would not be a good idea." Maddie snapped back to attention, only to have Eric breathing down her neck.

"Why not?"

"Well, I hate you for one. Two, it's not due until January. And three, I am busy tonight."

"I know, I know, the football game and the party," Eric said, "But I mean Saturday."

Maddie decided to end the conversation in order to stop Eric from following her to lunch after the bell rang to end the class. "Listen. It's nice to want to make it look like you want to do some work. Really, it is. But when I do the project, I'll just put your name on it."

"No way. I don't roll that way…anymore. I'll be at your house at eight p.m. sharp, on Saturday," Eric laughed as he jogged to meet up with some fellow jocks.

"Do you even know where I live?" Maddie yelled down the hall, not really expecting or wanting an answer. But Eric turned around and just gave two thumbs up, "I'll take that as a yes," she muttered.

"Everyone knows where you live. Just follow the trash trucks on Friday mornings, in case you forget," sneered Alexis from behind her.

After hearing a fit of giggles explode from behind her, Maddie spun around to face her arch-enemy but was surprised to find Alexis smiling sweetly with her eyes shining bright. Alongside Alexis was her simple-minded bestie,

Hannah Heston. Hannah was usually quiet, but when she spoke most people ignored her, simply because she had the mind of an eight-year-old. That being said, everyone actually liked Hannah, including Maddie. Her short poker-straight blonde hair added to her sweet appearance and although quite dumb, Maddie never heard her speak ill of anyone.

"Cornelious!" Alexis gushed, "We haven't really had any chance to talk this year."

Stepping up to the group of girls, Cornelious smiled, "Uh yeah, it's been a busy year so far. Hey Hannah."

"Did you know high school isn't even the highest school level? There's still four more years after it. I think I'm done after this school though. It's too much brain-thinking."

The three just stared at her, while she played with her hair. Cornelious turned to face Maddie, "So, was Eric giving you a hard time?"

"Not really. We're partners for that Econ project."

"What a coincidence, Cornelious and I are Bio partners," interjected the nuisance known as Alexis.

"Aren't there four lab partners to a group? And I'm in that group too," Maddie answered getting annoyed. "Plus, don't you have somewhere to go? I think a house just fell on your sister or something."

Cornelious and Hannah laughed, but Alexis just stuck her nose high in the air, pulled Hannah to her side, and strut off to wherever she felt was important. For the life of her, Maddie could not understand why any of her friends actually liked Alexis. But seeing as Carly and she cheered together for years, Alexis was a necessary evil at birthday parties and nearly every event growing up.

"You know Alexis isn't pure evil, as you like to think," Cornelious told Maddie, as if reading her mind.

"Yeah, yeah. That's what you guys all say. But I know the true Alexis Johnson. Anyway, I won't be at lunch. I'm meeting with Ms. Moskow.

"Wait. Why?"

But it was no use for Maddie was already halfway up the staircase.

****

Seeing as there were tests in both history and biology today, study hall presented the first opportunity for Cornelius to talk to Maddie all afternoon. "Lunch was horrible," Cornelious whispered to Maddie as she sat beside him in study hall. "I hope you had fun, cuz you left me in hell."

"Sorry, but I had to ask if she would be my advisor for selecting courses and eventually college."

"College already? We just got into high school."

"I like to be prepared," and I needed a break from those two, Maddie thought.

But before Cornelious could question her any further, he was interrupted.

"Are you guys talking about us?" Carly suddenly demanded.

"Because if you are, I just wanted to let you know that everything's fine. We're friends again and what not." Carly slid into her seat looking less frazzled and calmer than she had all week.

"Yeah, we realized there's no reason for us to be angry," Pilot added slowly but looked miserable.

"Okay, good. Because you two have been driving us mad," Cornelious said.

"So, Pilot, do you have the key-in code for me to breach security with?" Maddie asked rather slyly, hoping to get started with the investigation.

"Yup," Pilot nodded as he slid a crumpled piece of paper toward Maddie.

10

"And this is where we do the majority of our dining," Kirk motioned toward the oversized titanium kitchen as he passed. Kirk could not believe he was giving the grand tour of his house to his beloved Carly. Surely it was a dream when she asked him out. Kirk always thought there was something between her and that red-headed computer nerd. For once, he was glad to be wrong. On the other hand, Carly could not believe she was getting a grand tour of Kirk's house from, well, Kirk. This is the same Kirk who came to class in the third grade dressed as baby cupid and shot her in the back of the head with an arrow (suction cup---not real), proclaiming his undying love for her. Needless to say, the kid was creepy.

Charlie's Angels, she kept reminding herself. Just be like

Cameron Diaz from Charlie's Angels. "You must be getting this question a lot lately, but I was just wondering...where exactly did the thief sneak in?" Carly asked, playing with her hair to add emphasis to her good-natured manner.

"Well, I really shouldn't be showing you this, but I just can't say no to you, now can I, darling?" Kirk led Carly into a cozy room with two large bookshelves and a colossal fireplace. "We believe he came in through this window, for everything that was stolen was located in here," Kirk gestured with his arms held wide open.

Carly decided she would do a little sleuthing of her own, but all she managed to find was some cat hairs, and gum wrappers on the floor. Not to mention a baby picture of Kirk, dressed in old-fashioned garb as if he was alive in colonial times. Weird.

"I didn't know you have a cat," Carly said in reference to the cat hairs.

"That's because we don't silly, my mom's afraid of all things feline," Kirk shook his head and laughed as if he thought Carly was messing around.

"That's odd," Carly considered. "Not to complain, but shouldn't you have security with such a big house?" Carly asked giving her sweetest smile.

"We do, and it is funny you should ask, for that is the very next room on your right," he pointed, adding emphasis on the blazing red DO NOT ENTER sign. "I'll show you around real quick if you don't tell anyone what secrets lie within," laughed Kirk. He opened the door, and they entered a silver room with a gazillion buttons and about a dozen screens all aimed at different points of entry into the house. "No one can sneak in here, not even you," Kirk winked.

Not knowing how to answer, Carly simply laughed in reply, but was sure to jam the door on the way out, just as she had practiced with Maddie. All she had to do was stick a little wad of self-hardening silly-puddy in the lock-jam to prevent it from locking.

"Now, how about we watch a movie? Frankenstein sound inviting?"

"Um, sure Kirk. I'll just go to the bathroom and you pop the movie right in," Carly smiled and hurried to the bathroom. Once she was sure she was safely away from Kirk, she crossed over to the side of the house and opened a small window---just enough for Maddie to slip in undetected.

Either windows are getting smaller, or I'm getting bigger," Maddie groaned as she slipped into the Lomlings. Without a second's hesitation, Maddie entered the security room and typed in the key-code (that Pilot had provided). After watching the video five or six times, she decided it would be best to copy it and review it more diligently at home, where she wasn't so pressured. However, Maddie decided to watch it one more time---while a copy was being made. Besides the cleaning crew, all she noticed was a grainy and almost completely blacked out silhouette knocking on the door asking for or saying something and then entering the house. But the person, she concluded, was definitely not Kirk. "Oh crap," she thought as her alarm went off on her watch, "time to save Carly." Maddie grabbed the copy of the security tape, and quickly exited the house, only to come around front and knock on the door.

Kirk answered and wondered why in the world Maddie Petrozza would be standing on his front porch. But before he could ask, Carly was pushing her way past him, trying to explain how it was past her curfew and Maddie was here to take her home.

"We should do this again!" called Kirk from his doorway.

"See you in school!" came Carly's reply as she grabbed onto Maddie and the two girls sped down the darkened street, and into the gated community of Caldwell Courts. It was easy to spot Carly's spacious neo-colonial style house because it was the only one with all the lights on and Mrs. Cosentino waiting outside. Plus, from the inside, it was the only one that looked lived in (and yes, the gang had snuck into the other houses of Caldwell Courts to test this hypothesis).

"Perfect timing, I just made a batch of fudge-filled brownies," Mrs. Cosentino offered the girls.

"What a great night!" Maddie remarked as they laughed about Kirk and his undying love for Carly.

****

Whoever said high school was full of wild and crazy parties obviously wasn't at this one. Though Chase Shacklin had a pretty big house, an insane car collection, and an awesome indoor pool, everyone was content with standing around and talking, well standing around and drinking would be a more accurate description. Cornelious looked over and was glad to see someone was as bored as he was, even if it happened to be Pilot. Though coming with Rachel made the guys on his team respect him, or so some said, all he wanted to do was leave. Yes, Rachel was pretty, but she was actually quite vain, and wouldn't stop talking about her looks and complaining about soccer. Honestly, it was almost November and if you weren't starting by now, there was no way you would be by playoffs.

Cornelious told Pilot he'd be right back and headed to the bathroom. After a few minutes and wrong turns, Cornelious had to admit he was lost.

"Are you lost?" chuckled a familiar voice.

"Actually, Trent, I don't even know why I agreed to come to this party in the first place," Cornelious answered honestly.

Trent laughed, but his date answered, "It's because Rachel asked you to, and guys usually do what she wants."

"Hey...Mia. You know there's only one girl I listen to," Trent told his date as he pulled her closer to him.

"Nowadays, but you used to date her last year."

"That was one week, and I broke up with her."

"Which is exactly why she still---" but Trent pulled her lips to his and silenced Mia instantly.

Realizing they had been drawn into their own world, Cornelious said he had to go and uncomfortably slipped away. As he walked back down the stairs he saw Jason standing in the corner surrounded by a group of drunk and giddy Juniors, all feeling his mohawk. Seeing Cornelious he mouthed, "Long live the Mohawk." Cornelious just nodded and wondered when Jason had become such a toolbag. But then he realized it was probably since birth when he uttered his first word---which he told everyone it was 'HOT STUFF.' Maddie had pointed out that was two words, and Jason had called her know-it-all---the two were like oil and water.

When he came back to more familiar territory Cornelious decided it was time for Pilot and him to make a quick exit. But before he could grab Pilot and run for it, he was interrupted.

"Hey sssssshhhhhugar, I'vvvvveeee been looking allllll over for youuuuu," Rachel slurred as she hung onto Cornelious' shoulder. Slowly, she began to pull him towards the grand staircase, where some unfortunate person had fallen asleep with his shoes on and had permanent marker all over his face as a consequence. "Ya knooowww, I can get usssss a roooom upstairsssss..."

"Um, that's nice and all...but you're drunk and I gotta go."

"But youuuuu can't ggooo," Rachel purred. "And I'mm not drunk...Nina annnnd I are only on round two."

"Honestly, I don't know what I was thinking. Do you want me to take you home or call you an uber?" Cornelious desperately wanted to leave, but felt uncomfortable leaving Rachel when she was drinking.

"Ha! I neverr leave partiesss before midnight! Don't you knowww, who I ammm?" Rachel smugly crossed her arms, and smiled enticingly.

Cornelious backed up, and told her he really had to go. When she started making a scene, pulling some of her friends around her, Cornelious tried one more time to politely explain that he was leaving. When she still didn't want to hear it, he decided to tell her the truth and said, "I'm just not into this party, honestly. And I don't think you're my type…so, I'll just see you around, okay?"

"I'mmm not your type?! I'mmm everyone's type! We jussstt neeeeed to bbeeee alone," Rachel wiggled her eyebrows and beckoned him over to her.

Cornelious, having no desire to be alone with Rachel, didn't even bother to say goodbye, as he latched onto Pilot and they dashed out the glass doors.

"When we tell the girls how tonight went," Pilot began, "let's say it was awesome and we never had so much fun in our lives."

"Deal," Cornelious agreed wholeheartedly. In the distance, Pilot and Cornelious heard sirens and laughed over the fact that they had just missed the po-po busting the party.

11

When the sound of an expensive convertible pulled up in front of the Petrozza household midday Saturday, a tired Mrs. Petrozza opened the door and simply pointed down the street. For Carly and Cornelious, who were passengers in Mia's car but very eager to reach the end of their hazardous ride, this was a simple gesture meaning the kids were helping their father at the shop. Before Mia could speed away, a struggling Pilot leapt from the doorway of his house and sprinted to the car.

"PILOT!" came the boom of his mother's voice, "I TOLD YOU THAT YOU ARE NOT TO LEAVE UNTIL YOU CLEAN THE DOWNSTAIRS!"

"SORRY MOM, CAN'T HEAR YA!" boomed a reply, as Pilot strapped himself in, made the sign of the cross, and closed his eyes tight, as the speedy convertible made its way perilously down the road. Carly could tell her sister was excited to get to the shop, but not for the same reason they were. Mia had told her parents earlier that morning that her car needed tweaking, for she kept getting speeding tickets. Carly had murmured that perhaps Asbury's driving school needed tweaking, but knew that the real reason she was going to the shop was to get more than just her car looked at.

Arriving before a greased-up blue and gold mechanic shop, with rusty off-blue lettering reading: 'PETROZZA AUTO---WHERE YOU AUTO GO'---Mia's car screeched to a stop, alerting everyone that she had arrived. The Petrozza clan literally popped out from every nook and cranny the store held.

"CORNELIOUS!" called two very dirty twins, as they ran toward him with their arms outstretched. Cornelious tried to dodge them, but unfortunately for Cornelious, they were quicker and knocked him to the floor. Alec walked slowly out of the front garage doors and sparked up a conversation with Pilot over the previous night's season finale to some Sci-Fi show. Carly looked over to find Sophia looking a little more than embarrassed, and felt it was necessary to speak with her. In the Petrozza family pretty much everyone was tough as nails, that is, except for Sophia. Though she was in no way lazy, she preferred to hang out with her gal pals or go to the boardwalk---anything other than fiddling with various car parts. Cornelious looked over to see Trent leaning beside Mia, with his shirt off, of course. Cornelious had to admit it, Trent knew how to get the ladies' attention---

"Hey, where's Maddie?" Pilot interrupted Cornelious' thoughts.

"She's helping dad rebuild that '54 Pontiac Bonneville Special Motorama Concept Car," Trent replied. Then, when nobody understood his lingo he added with a chuckle, "You know, that really old green racing car with the windows that open upward and the chrome rims."

Nodding, the gang understood and walked to the back lot of the shop to see a grease-stained Mr. Petrozza underneath the car, and Maddie leaning under the front hood.

"I think that it will, or rather, could be up and running soon, Old Man," Maddie laughed.

"I don't know, but I sure hope so Little Girly," Mr. Petrozza chuckled.

"Yeah, Little Girly, I hope so too," Cornelious spoke as he snuck up behind Maddie.

Realizing others were there, she spun around and ended up banging her head against the hood.

"OW! Hey! How long have you creepers been here?" Maddie asked rubbing her head while trying, in vain, to wipe the oil off her face.

"Only a few seconds really," Carly smiled.

"Dad, would it be possible for me to leave? I really have some urgent business to attend to..." Maddie batted her eyes and gave her best puppy-dog face to her father. In the end,

the broad-shouldered two-time-high-school-state-
championship-baseball star could not resist and told them
they could leave if they brought Sophia and the twins with
them. Seeing no other option, Maddie agreed.

"I call riding on Cornelious' back!" Shannon cried.

"Aw, whatever. After all, he is your BOYFRIEND!"
Daniel stated, but then had to run as a raging Shannon chased
him down the road and right into their house. Before Mrs.
Petrozza could get her bearings, four grimy children entered
the house (she had just finished cleaning), while three clean
ones tried to creep up the stairs.

"Maddie.........."

"Dad, told me to take them home. Sophia will shower
after I make sure the twins shower. And then I--er, we have
important things to do...so please don't bother us." Maddie
quickly told her mom as she shooed the children upstairs.

Knowing how long it would take to get the twins, as well
as herself, showered, Maddie told the gang to chill in her
room. By the time everyone was settled it was almost eight.
While they were waiting, Cornelious went downstairs to
measure the food supply. Unsurprisingly, there was barely
any. Making sure no one saw or heard him, he quickly dialed
Brady's and basically ordered a truckload of tacos, nachos,
and soda---then he asked if it was possible for them to throw
in a gallon of milk (for Maddie who absolutely despised soda),
and added he would pay extra. Thus, when Maddie was fully
changed and ready, she came downstairs to find her family
and friends feasting on a delicious meal. As usual, Cornelious

acted as if Maddie had paid for everything (with what money? Maddie thought), and left a seat open for her with a tall glass of milk waiting. Though she hated looking like a charity case, Maddie knew it was impossible to say no to milk and Brady's tacos.

When they had finished eating, the gang hurriedly went upstairs to Maddie's room and locked the door. Maddie walked over to the newly-purchased (thanks to Carly) easel and giant writing pad, where the basic information of the crime was already bulleted.

"Okay, so first off---" Maddie began.

"How was the party?" Carly asked.

"It was the most fu---" Cornelious started his rehearsed line.

"It was dreadfully boring, you girls were right," Pilot confessed.

At this, Carly did not even try to conceal her smile, as she looked from guy to guy.

"Getting back to the point," Maddie tapped the notes, "On one of the tapes---

This time Maddie wasn't interrupted by one of her friends, but rather it was her mother yelling for Maddie to come downstairs and greet her guest. Maddie had no clue who could possibly be at her house on a Saturday night and said as much to her mother as her friends followed her down to the kitchen.

"It's a cute boy! I knew that's why you were so happy the other day!" Mrs. Petrozza beamed.

"What? Who?!" both Maddie and Carly asked.

"Hey, I didn't know there was a party going on. I would have brought my dancing shoes," joked a familiar blonde-haired boy in a green polo, who had his back to the gang and was busy taking a bite of a cold taco.

"Eric? What are you doing---Oh crap! I told you I was busy. Can't we reschedule?"

"Honey, that is no way to treat a guest who has traveled across town to see you," Mrs. Petrozza stated disapprovingly. "So did you two meet this year? Maddie never talks about any boys, except those two that is." Mrs. Petrozza gestured nonchalantly to Pilot and Cornelious, and offered Eric a seat.

"Okay, okay. You're right, just let me talk to him outside. Alone," Maddie added as her friends, and mother, began to follow her.

Maddie shut the front door behind her, even though she knew everyone was probably watching anyway. "Can we seriously reschedule? I mean this project isn't due until the end of the term. And I have some serious matters at hand."

"Seriously? Well, okay. But we are doing this project together."

"Okay, okay I get it. I can't see why you're trying so hard to do the work when all you ever do is complain."

"That was the old me, this is the new and improved me. Like when they replaced Katie Holmes with Maggie Gyllenhaal in Batman."

"That was not an improvement, that was a serious downgrade," Maddie laughed, but then caught herself. There was no way she would make nice with someone who had almost gotten her expelled from school.

"Aha! See! I think we have more in common than you know. But before you can say anything, I'm going to leave. See ya around," Eric added as he swiftly jumped on his bike and rode back to where he, and his expensive ride, belong.

****

When everything had finally settled down and there were no more surprises, the group put their heads together and began to review the case. Maddie had finished telling the gang that she saw the silhouette of what she thought was (the size of) a teenage boy linger at the door and enter the house. However, the tapes didn't show him exiting so she never got a chance to see his face---to general dismay.

"Well, I saw some stray cat hairs," Carly added when she saw the group was looking a little glum.

"So what? They have cats," Pilot added, plopping down onto one of Maddie's oversized beanie-bags.

"No, Mr. Smarty Pants, they do NOT have cats," Carly chided. "Which is precisely why I think it's so strange that in the room where the theft occurred, cat hair was evident."

"You're right Carly," Cornelious announced. "Maybe the robber has a pet cat, and the hairs fell off his jacket."

"Pilot, would you be able to come up with a list of students at Asbury who have cats?" Maddie asked.

"Sure, if you want a list longer than the Nile," Pilot yawned.

Looking at Pilot curled up on the bean-bag yawning made

everyone laugh, but also, in turn, yawn. Therefore, the group decided to call it a night and pick up where they left off later.

12

In most towns around the country, Halloween is known to all and loved by many as a holiday in which young children enjoy procuring candy, and then throwing it up hours later after stuffing themselves. In the town of Asbury, there is another more affluent tradition that occurs on this day every year.

"Our Halloween Ball shall be the best yet!" boomed Jeremiah Gibbz over the loudspeaker at the break of dawn, successfully waking up Cornelious. "Cornelious! Nancy! Up and at 'em! We have a big day ahead of us!"

How could Halloween, become my least favorite holiday in a matter of years? Cornelious asked himself. But then he remembered the answer: his father. Usually the rich use Thanksgiving and Christmas as an excuse to exploit their loved ones. Jeremiah Gibbz however, used every holiday or chance he could find. Thus, a few years back it was decided a Governor's ball, or rather Jeremiah Gibbz's ball, was to be held every Halloween evening with a mandatory attendance--- for those who could afford it. West Asburyans were encouraged to attend, but most couldn't afford it or simply worked at the ball.

Cornelious got out of bed and looked out his window at the West-Siders' domain. Pilot and Maddie are so lucky all they have to do is work, and not talk to 'everyone of importance', Cornelious thought as he turned from the window and walked down the stairs to prepare.

****

"Ahh! Cornelious and Carly are so lucky! They can just dress up and relax. While you and I have to help cater the darn party," Maddie was pacing back and forth in her room, while Pilot was aimlessly infiltrating Britain's government, via his tablet.

"Hey, I know who's gonna be the next Prime Minister...Oh I mean, Maddie, it's not that bad. I mean, do you think Mr. Gibbz would let us in otherwise?"

"Honestly, Pilot? He wouldn't even notice you, sorry. But he would find me and throw me out. Even if I was wearing Harry Potter's invisibility cloak."

Pilot laughed as he looked up from his laptop, and realized his friend was truly stressing out. "You're right, you're right…say, what are we wearing? I mean last year we were kitty caterers, remember?"

"How could I possibly forget that? I'm still coughing up fur balls."

Pilot always knew how to turn a bad situation into a good one, and Maddie was glad she wasn't going to be working the ball alone tonight.

"Well, I think the theme is creatures of the night or something."

"This…should be interesting."

****

When Asbury was originally founded there were seven wealthy families who believed money is the foundation for life. Therefore, it was no surprise when they formed a society called "Parcels of Pecunia," to promote prestige. In layman's terms, the society's name is "Members of Money," Pecunia meaning money in Latin. Clearly, it was no surprise that one of the first projects they underwent was the construction of the massive banquet hall, Pecunia Palace---clearly they thought hard for a while when naming that one. Anyway, it was their belief that celebrations should be for the wealthy, and therefore should be hosted in a splendid building. The ancestors of the Parcels of Pecunia still reside in East Asbury and partake in the organization and all of its activities. Jeremiah Gibbz may not have family ties to the Parcels, but he surely has enough money to rent out the Palace a few times each year.

Jeremiah decided that although last year may have been a

cute theme, mostly to satisfy his wife, this year he had to spice things up. Therefore, Creatures of The Night was a theme that wasn't too scary nor cute, and (as an added bonus) enabled him to poke fun at his political rivals, by hanging their photos next to monsters on the walls of the Palace. Before letting the Help in (much to his chagrin two of Cornelious' friends were included in that category), he had to make sure everything was perfect. Blood-colored punch sat on every table, real cobwebs were placed in the high-ceiling corners, and the floor was covered with dust, mud, and even fake insects. Nooses hung from the rafters, all railings in the building were covered with an unknown sticky substance, and the bathrooms had smoke pouring out of them---health inspectors were clearly paid off.

Now all I have to do is ensure that Cornelious only talks to those who matter, Jeremiah thought as he glanced at the dreadfully mischievous window art.

Guests were set to arrive around seven, which meant that Maddie and Pilot were to be in the ballroom two hours prior, which further meant they were dressed like 'The Creature from The Black Lagoon' for the past three hours.

"I know last year's theme was 'cute to boot' and all, but why this drastic change?"

Maddie looked at her outfit and laughed because Pilot, as usual, was right on the money. As for their catering uniforms, this year they all wore dark leotards (I know, why?!), with seaweed and a mud-like substance covering every inch of their clothing, except their 'serving-hands' as Mr. Gibbz liked to call them.

"I think we're supposed to be The Creature from the Black Lagoon Caterers, which still makes no sense. But as long I get twenty-five an hour—for the next seven hours---I'm all good."

"Maybe then I can buy my new adaptor or code encryptor! I've been saving up for lo---"

Maddie was about to smack Pilot but he stopped short anyway. There is only one thing, or rather person, that could stop Pilot from talking 'tech.' So, Maddie knew that the Cosentinos had arrived. "We're not literally supposed to be creatures from the black lagoon," Maddie whispered and motioned to Pilot's mouth, "You drooling all over only makes us look worse!"

"Oh shut up. I wasn't drooling," then on second thought, "at least not noticeably, right?"

Maddie chuckled and picked up her tray to begin serving the richie-riches. She quickly made her way over to the Cosentinos.

"I'll have the crab cakes, please. Oh, I didn't recognize you, darling."

"It's fine, I think that's the whole point, Mrs. Cosentino."

"Oh, can I snap a few quick pics?" the world-renowned photographer excitedly asked, stepping between his wife and Maddie.

"Okay Mr. Cosentino, but make it quick, us creatures don't like to be kept waiting. Or rather the monster who pays us doesn't."

Both Cosentinos laughed and took some quick snapshots. Hoping the photos didn't end up in the annual Halloween Ball Bonanza Magazine, Maddie turned and went over to where Pilot and Carly were deep in conversation.

"Well, I'm obviously a vampire."

"Really? Because you just look like a regular person to me, in really expensive clothes that is."

"That's the whole point. Everyone knows vampires are sexy, right Mads?"

Looking at Carly's semi-short blue dress, and diamond, well, everything, Maddie had to agree with Pilot. "Sorry Car, but it just looks like you're heading to a party. Don't vamps wear capes and brooches?"

"Wow. Okay Dracula. I'm talking about the new-age vampires. Never mind, it's not even worth it," Carly decided to give up the fight, exasperated over having to defend her 'costume'.

"Ya know, it doesn't even matter. It's not like the Gibbzs dress up. They just look all fancy, as usual," Maddie added, with perfect timing. For as she spoke, the Gibbz family arrived at the top of the staircase, and were slowly descending. Each member beamed and looked like a million bucks, or probably more appropriately, a billion bucks. Maddie gave Neal a head nod, but knew that was probably the only communication they would have for the night, after all he has to make the proper impression.

"Cornelious, remember, tonight is important," Jeremiah hissed through a clenched, yet perfectly smiling jaw.

"I know, father," Cornelious managed to say through his beaming smile. Descending the stairs, smiling the whole time, Cornelious managed to find his friends and return a head nod and a real smile. Making his way around the room, he realized the costumes were improving each year. In fact, some people he honestly couldn't recognize.

"Hey cutie, who are you supposed to be?"

Cornelious turned to face Alexis Johnson, who didn't look half bad. She wore a short black and white velvet dress, and was wearing a black wig with a long white streak. "Frankenstein's wife?"

"I should've known you would guess. Can you believe no one else knew? I'm pretty sure almost everyone is a vampire."

As Alexis said this, Carly walked by and added, "Well, some people look good as vampires."

Cornelious laughed and saw his best friend sidling by. Smirking, he called "Waiter!"

"We prefer Creature tonight," Maddie laughed handing him a Coke. Cornelious downed it and was about to ask for another one, when his father pulled him away.

"I thought I told you to---

"I know, sir. I was just getting a drink. Sir."

"Well don't...Isn't that your new counselor?" Cornelious looked over to where his father was pointing, and nodded. "Well, she sure is pretty."

Cornelious waited until his father went to mingle, before greeting Ms. Clarke. In a long red dress, with her long brown hair all tied up, Ms. Clarke did look quite pretty. Not wanting to interrupt her conversation with Rodney, his fellow teammate, he was about to turn around when she spotted him. Rodney exchanged hellos with Cornelious before heading over to the refreshment table to talk to his present girlfriend.

"Well, hello Cornelious. Quite a party you have here, huh?"

"Yes, ma'am. You look lovely."

"Why, thank you. Do you know who I am tonight?"

"Uh...a vampire?"

"Good heavens no. I think that trend has gone a bit too far."

"Actually, I think it's a trend that will always remain fashionable," Carly stated as she passed by, evidently hearing their conversation as well.

After arching her eyebrows in the direction of Carly, Ms. Clarke continued on, "Anyway, I chose to be Persephone. Hades' imprisoned wife in the Underworld."

"Oh. Well, that's...er...tragic." Cornelious honestly did not know how to reply.

"Yes, but also poetic."

Luckily, another student came over to say hello, and Cornelious found an opening to leave.

"Hey Jason, who are you supposed to be...IT?"

"No. John Wayne Gacy the serial killer, aka The Killer Clown." Jason told Cornelious this fact as if everyone knew all about Gacy. Cornelious was about to ask him another question, when Jason suddenly smiled.

"OH WAITER!" Jason Scott called over to Maddie. "I need another 7-Up this one is quite dry."

"That doesn't even make sense," Maddie added as she poured another 7-Up into the killer clown's mug.

"Aren't you supposed to be in costume at this event?" Jason laughed.

"Come on man, be nice," Cornelious uttered.

"I think she is in costume, aren't you Maddie?" Hannah looked like someone had asked her to explain the Quadratic Formula.

"Yes, Hannah. Jason was just making a joke," Maddie stated, and turned to pour drinks elsewhere.

"I was?" Jason smirked.

Clueless as usual, Hannah declared, "This is a confusing conversation, I'm gonna go find someone cute to talk to."

"You know..." Jason began, as everyone around him groaned, knowing that some of pointless bragging was next, "...my great-great-great grandfather, Ryan Scott, founded Asbury and began the Parcels of Pecunia."

Maddie visibly rolled her eyes, as Cornelious stifled his own groan. But Jason didn't seem to notice and continued, as usual. "I even have his old ring with the Pecunia crest right on it." Jason held out his hand for all to admire a lady in white dress, holding a golden shield and a golden staff, with a full moon visible in the background---all impossibly etched on a large golden ring.

"I know what you're thinking. It's a lot of detail on just one piece of jewelry. In fact, it's probably more than both of your houses put together," Jason laughed indicating both Pilot and Maddie.

"I was actually thinking that it would suck to have to hold a golden shield and staff all of the time. And what do they say about those with large jewelry...that they're trying to compensate for something they're lacking?" Maddie replied innocently smiling.

Before Cornelious could hear Jason's reply, Jeremiah Gibbz boomed from across the room: "Cornelious boy, come over here I want you to meet someone important."

Cornelious marched over to his father and checked his wristwatch, wishing Halloween could be fun and not just another photo op.

The party wore on throughout the night, and by two in the morning the Palace was officially empty. Jeremiah Gibbz had invited some people back to the mansion, so when Mrs. Petrozza offered to take everyone back to their house, no one refused. Cornelious and Maddie dragged themselves to Maddie's room and crashed on her bed. Carly, however, was so exhausted; she couldn't even make it out of the car, leaving Pilot to carry her into Maddie's room.

"I thought vampires could fly." Pilot managed to say, before laying Carly down on the bean bag and passing out on the floor right next to her.

13

Trent burst into Maddie's room at the break of dawn revealing that the Wallabee's had been robbed during the night. Before Trent could give the scant details, the foursome was up and ready to go. They decided the best course of action would be to bike down to the Wallabee's, before the police arrived and tainted the evidence. The group darted to the shed between Pilot and Maddie's houses, and grabbed four bikes before heading up to East Asbury. Though they arrived pretty quickly, the police were on the scene and were adamant about keeping the accumulating crowd at bay.

Coincidentally, Mia had been friends with Marissa Wallabee growing up, so Carly knew how to sneak into the house undetected. Waiting until the cops were distracted by the crowd, the gang chose the perfect moment to sneak away. Carly, Pilot, Cornelious, and Maddie snuck over to the side of the house where a large oak was situated. Briskly shimmying up the tree, they managed to climb into an open window, and into the master bathroom. Because the family was downstairs being questioned by police, they were safe to roam the upstairs in hopes of finding a secure place to eavesdrop. Having no such luck, they stealthly made their way down the stairs, and as some officers passed by, slipped into the broom closet in the nick of time.

"So, Mr. Wallabee---" began an officer, who looked more like a Chippendale worker than a Justice Department employee---in fact, he even walked around as if he was performing an elaborate dance routine, sidestepping furniture and pointing to various items.

"James. Mr. Wallabee is my father's name," retorted a very stressed out Mr. James Wallabee. "And just what is your name, officer?"

"Officer Chip."

"Classic, I could have guessed that," Pilot whispered, and the gang nodded in agreement.

"Er, James... you say you were out last night, returned home, and immediately retired to bed?" Officer Chip, as he was duly named, now paced about the room looking more like a CSI actor than an actual officer.

"Yes. My Claire loves to dance, and we happened to enjoy ourselves last night. When we arrived home we were extremely tired." James remarked, all the while wringing his hands, and trying desperately to keep his eyes open.

"Okay. So, let's review yesterday's events one more time, shall we?"

"If we must," was the tired reply.

"So, you woke up and had breakfast..."

"Yes, yes. Breakfast. I did some bills, while Claire took the kids to daycare. The cleaning crew came around one and left around three or three thirty. Then we had a late lunch and went off to the annual Governor's Halloween Ball around eight, only to return around one, maybe two."

"So, that leaves us a possible six-hour window, hmm..." the officer got up and examined the room. "And, all in all, not much was stolen, correct? Only about six grand?"

"If you are inferring that a six-thousand-dollar theft is a miniscule amount---"

"Of course not, it's just with a house of this size, I would think more would be stolen. Maybe the thief didn't want to arouse suspicion and thought that by only taking a small amount now, they could return to take more later," the officer concluded, clearly quite proud of his logic.

"Oh. I think understand your reasoning...but who could do such a thing? And who would even be able to, on a regular basis?"

"Well, doesn't a cleaning service come around quite often?" implied the officer.

"Actually...yes. And they do come around on a regular basis. Natalie Petrozza's business. They do a rather thorough job too…you're not suggesting that she had any---"

"As of yet, we have no proof of anything. Just suspicions, just suspicions."

"What?" Maddie whispered incredulously. "That's my mom's business they're talking about. No way is she going to be the scapegoat!"

Furiously, Maddie rose to refute the accusations against her mother, only to have Cornelious pull her down and caution, "Nobody's arresting your mom. There's no evidence. So just chill." Cornelious looked over at Maddie and knew that though he had managed to calm her down, she was still shaking and fury had spread to her eyes. Cornelious even had to clamp his hand over her mouth to keep her from protesting.

When the officers drifted away from the closet, the gang ran up the stairs, climbed down the tree, and sped away from the crime scene undetected. The group rode their bikes down to the beach to piece together the new information and try to decipher any clues they could derive from their current evidence. Before riding up onto the boardwalk Maddie pulled her bike to a stop, and shook with outrage. A general feeling of dread was building and the gang felt that things were about to get worse. Furthermore, they each knew this was no longer a laughing matter, and it was time to seriously step up their investigation.

"Okay guys, this is beginning to get more serious than I originally thought," Maddie stated averting her eyes from the group.

"True. We need to keep all of our eyes and ears open for more clues," Pilot chimed in, hoping Maddie would ease up a little.

"And we need to pick up the pace," Maddie concluded as she faced the group. "Whoever is doing this, is getting smarter. His thieveries increased in monetary values as well!"

"What?" Carly asked.

"I mean, he stole a larger amount this time," Maddie explained, clearly flustered.

Carly and Pilot glanced at each other and nervously waited for someone to break the silence.

"Plus, with no real suspects," Cornelious added for Maddie's sake, "there's no telling when this robber's reign will end."

"Unless he waits until your mom's arrested to end his streak and make a clean break for it," Pilot added.

"Not helping," Carly snapped.

"True, but at least we have motivation now," Cornelious added.

"Yeah, but that's about all we have," Maddie stated, as they got on their bikes and tried to sort out the facts.

14

"One of the trickiest yet most self-satisfying things you can ever do," began the slender teacher, "is to leave no trace behind."

"Obviously! That's why you always use a rubber!" boasted the most obnoxious freshman and perhaps even student at Asbury High, Ed.

"How telling that you should be the one to attempt a joke," remarked Ms. Catharziniolasheyos, or as she is more commonly referred to, Cat.

Looking at Cat, Maddie wondered how she could possibly be in her thirties and unmarried. She truly was the best-looking female teacher at Asbury, all the students admitted it.

With her sleek black hair extending past her shoulders, and her blue almond shaped eyes sparkling atop her perfect olive-skinned complexion, guys should have been falling all over her. And the male students at Asbury definitely were. However, rumor had it she had been engaged to the love of her life and could not have been happier. Then on the eve of her wedding night, her fiancé had revealed that he was going off to be with the true love of his life---her brother! Maddie could see how this would devastate anyone, and felt sorry for Cat whenever she would be seen eating or strolling around town alone.

"Maddie! That's it!" Cornelious snapped her back to attention, and she realized she had missed a crucial part of the lesson.

"Crap! I dozed off again. Now, I'm going to have to stay after and get caught up. Or maybe I should just read the book. I definitely can't get the notes from Alexis---"

"Shut up! I'll tell you what you missed because I was actually paying attention. And it really is important," Cornelious finished.

Maddie looked at him and couldn't believe this was the same kid she'd been giving her notes to for years when he fell asleep in class, or 'just didn't feel like taking notes that day.'

"What? Why are you smiling?" Cornelious questioned.

"Oh, uh, no reason," I've got to stop doing that, thought Maddie. "I was just thinking of how much you've grown."

"Wha---" But, as usual he was cut off by the bell, and Maddie and Cornelious made their way down to the library.

Study hall was being used for discussing the case, rather than actual studying. Their case conferences, as the group deemed them, were starting to affect their grades, well except for Maddie, who was working on maintaining her perfect 4.0 GPA. But unfortunately for Maddie, her high marks drew Cunningham's attention, and Maddie was pulled aside and asked to join book club. Knowing that participation in this club looked good on college résumés, coupled with the fact that Maddie truly enjoyed reading, left Maddie with no choice but to agree. However, she did ask Cunningham if it would be possible for her to join after soccer. Cunningham was so ecstatic at a new prospect she agreed to wait, as long as Maddie kept up on the readings.

"This is impossible," Maddie groaned.

"Don't say that, we'll clear your mom's name, don't worry."

"Thanks Neal, but I was talking about playoffs, school, this case, and now book club. Why did I agree? No, don't answer that."

"On that note…any other news?" Pilot queried.

"Well, Rodney Shiffler broke up with his girlfriend Julia Dougherty, which isn't a surprise seeing how he's been flying through girls this year. Oh! And apparently Sarah G. and Carly D. found out Paul B. was dating both of them!" Carly spewed out faster than anyone could comprehend.

"Carly. I love you and all, but you seriously have got diarrhea of the mouth," Maddie stated shaking her head.

"Yes, well that was interesting, but is there any news on

the homefront aka," Pilot paused to lean in and whisper, "the case?"

Maddie turned to Cornelious, who was so beside himself with pride, he appeared to have just solved the cure for the common cold.

"Well, for those of you who have been paying attention to anything Cat has instructed us on today---"

"Just tell us already," Carly complained.

"Nah, give him his moment of glory. Look how excited he is, I'll be surprised if he doesn't wet himself," Maddie smirked, leaning on her hand to bask in the glow of Cornelious' pure pride.

"Well, if that's how it's gonna be..." Cornelious paused and then continued, "Cat's lesson today taught us how to eliminate our fingerprints."

"What? How's that possible?" Maddie was intrigued, and by glancing at Pilot and Carly, she could tell they were more than interested.

"Cat told us that she really shouldn't be teaching us this, but it has always interested her, and she wanted to show us how fun science could be. Ya know, the usual bull," Cornelious chuckled.

"But how exactly?" Maddie whispered, irritated she didn't have the answer for once, and had to wait for someone to explain it to her.

"Cat said by using fine grit sandpaper--which is stored in our woodshop class and local department stores as well---you simply have to sand your fingertips away."

"Ouch! That's got to kill!" Carly shrieked looking down at her well-manicured hands.

Cornelious continued on, addressing this point and how it wouldn't pose a threat, "No. That's what I originally thought too. The thing is, it DOESN'T hurt at all. Unless you have an allergic reaction, in which case your fingertips would turn itchy and red."

"But are you sure sanding off your skin wouldn't hurt? How's that possible?" Pilot wondered.

"Yes. It wouldn't or rather couldn't hurt even a little bit because----"

"Because you're just scraping away dead skins cells and not the nerves!" Maddie finished smiling.

"I thought you weren't paying attention," Cornelious stated, disheartened.

"I wasn't but that's just common sense. How could I not see this?! But," Maddie added as she saw Cornelious' pride take a hit, "if it wasn't for you we wouldn't have known how the robber is leaving behind no traces."

"Well, couldn't he be wearing gloves?" Carly asked, while mentally picturing all the people of Asbury who frequently wear gloves.

"No." Maddie said firmly, "this robber must've known the cops would check to see who has recently purchased gloves, while testing the crime scenes for latex and other materials--- all of which has turned up negative," Maddie affirmed. "Which we know thanks to Pilot cracking the Police Database."

"Which is so easy, I basically did it in my sleep," Pilot added glancing at Carly.

"Nobody likes a bragger," Carly responded.

"Is that even a word?" Pilot shot back.

"Anyway…" Maddie interjected, before Cunningham had a reason to stop playing with her stuffed fox and shush the group.

"Anyway… the thief would also have to make sure they used new sandpaper every time, because this method only lasts for a few days." Cornelious told the gang.

"Now we have a couple of leads…maybe," Maddie realized.

"How so? I mean we know how, but where does that really lead us?" Carly inquired.

"If they knew about this method and used it, that means they attended Asbury High, or might actually still be in attendance. I mean, Cat did say she tells her class this method every year, as a way to keep her students interested in her class, and hopefully spark conversation."

"That leaves room for a lot of suspects," Carly stated.

"Even if the person graduated they had to have had Cat, and since she's only been teaching for eight years the thief is, at most, 26ish," Maddie calculated.

"Not if someone came home from school and told siblings or friends or anyone really about what they learned," Carly pointed out.

"How many high schoolers tell other people what they learned in school each day?" Cornelious argued.

"I'm saying it's possible, which would lead us nowhere," Carly decided.

"Okay Buzz Killington, I'm just saying, what if the perpetrator is among us now?" Maddie shot back.

"I don't know what's creepier," Pilot began, "the thief being a high-schooler who walks besides us virtually every day, or an old creeper who retains some knowledge from high school and uses it to break into people's houses."

"I'd have to say the first one is a lot creepier," Carly told Pilot as if he had just proposed the world's dumbest hypothesis.

"Anyway, if he still goes to Asbury we can check the woodshop and see who's borrowed or used sandpaper---" Pilot continued as if he hadn't heard Carly.

"Which is just about everyone in woodshop," Cornelious interjected.

15

Maddie may have found it difficult to focus completely on the game during warm-ups, but as soon as the refs blew their whistle, it was time to battle. Even though Asbury had a great season thus far, this playoff game was sure to be a literal bloodbath. Ever since the town was founded, and the high school was built, it seemed Mainland Regional High was created just to rival it in every aspect. A loss to Mainland Regional was as unacceptable as ordering plain frozen yogurt at Cold Stone Creamery---you just don't do it. Naturally, Asbury lost to Mainland once in a while. However, in grade school Cornelious and Maddie promised each other, as well as Dennis and Brandan at Brady's, that they would never lose to Mainland, no matter what.

Luckily, for Cornelious, Carly, and Pilot, they were free on Saturday morning and had the chance to watch the bloodbath. Two girls from Asbury and four from Mainland Regional were carried off the field. Truly, this was a highly anticipated game, for there wasn't a free seat in the bleachers.

"These games make me nervous. Do you think I should start a cheer?"

"Seriously, Carly? At a soccer game?" Pilot laughed.

"Yes, here! They should have the right to have cheerleaders too! But I guess that might be weird," Carly said on second thought.

"Man, I love soccer. Well girls soccer that is," Jason said, as he squeezed his way behind Carly.

"You love anything with the word 'girls' in it," Carly reputed.

"Well, they are my favorite thing to watch."

"That's because watching is the closest that girls let you get to them," Pilot responded.

While Carly laughed and latched onto Pilot's arm---making his face match his hair---Cornelious looked back and noticed Jason ball his fists.

"She's great at soccer, huh?" Eric interjected.

"I didn't even see you there dude. Sucks that you guys lost last night. That ends your season right?" Jason asked Eric, and Cornelious was glad for the distraction.

"Yeah, but now I can practice for basketball. I better make JV."

"You will. I need my three-guard after all," Cornelious joked.

"Dude, you're gonna be on Varsity, without a dou---OH MAN! WHAT A GREAT HEADER! WOOO-HOOO! GO MADDIE!"

The gang watched as the time clock ticked down to zero and a big smile fell across Maddie's otherwise exhausted face.

It felt better than waking up in Disney World when you realized you had just beaten Mainland. While trying to keep the promise to Dennis and Brandan, Maddie managed to procure a hattrick, and her third goal was an amazing header from a beautiful pass from fellow teammate Liz. The final was 5 to 3, but the play seemed to be about even. After the game, Maddie went over to join her friends.

"Hey, great job."

"Thanks, Jazz."

Before Maddie could ask about his upcoming concert, she was flanked on all sides by spectators and friends.

"Great job."

"That corner kick assist of yours was amazing."

"Oh Lovey! What a lovable game to win on such a lovable day!" (Easy to guess who said that, right?).

"Yeah, yeah. Good job. You could've had a fourth goal, if you didn't aim so far left."

"Thanks Ed."

"He's obnoxious, you played great!" Carly stated as she hugged her best friend.

"Great job Mads."

"Thanks Neal, now it's your turn," Maddie smiled.

****

"It's all tied up at the half folks! With Gibbz running in for two touchdowns for Asbury, and two Mainland slobs---I mean players (apparently even the announcer for the game had to abide by Principal Coste's strict guidelines), scoring a touchdown apiece."

"Whew, this game is intense," Maddie said as she sat down during the break in play.

"I can't believe they didn't call that unnecessary roughness penalty on 24, Trent got destroyed," Jazz remarked.

"Yeah, he'll be hurting for a while. I think the refs are too afraid to call anything, except the absolute obvious."

"Otherwise known as touchdowns."

"Isn't that uniform just so cute?" Pilot murmured.

"I guess Neal looks good, I never really thought of it," Maddie laughed.

"Ew. I meant Carly," Pilot stated as he enthusiastically waved to Carly.

"You should ask her out before someone else does," Jazz sagely told Pilot.

"What if she says no? I'll be humiliated."

Before the conversation could continue, the cheerleaders started going wild. Front and back flips were performed, and chants started up again. Which only meant one thing---part II of the game was about to begin. Throughout the second half, the play was fairly even. Unfortunately, Mainland was up by one field goal, and with barely any time left.

"Okay, Gibbz. 10 seconds left. We're down by three. We have to score now, or face humiliating defeat. Let's run Oklahoma 4," Rodney confidently told the team, as they huddled together to choose a play.

Feeling his face growing red, Cornelious thanked God for the helmet her was wearing. Looking over to the eager crowd, Cornelious spotted his father easily---a look of disappointment already poised on his face. Next to his father, his mother had actually brought the fat cat Howie. Classic mom. As he scanned the faces, he also picked out Maddie and Pilot, sitting with Jazz Peters---who was playing, yes playing, his guitar in the middle of the crowd. He realized Maddie was signaling to the far side of the field, near to where he was standing. Right away, Cornelious understood that Mainland was lining up heavy, on his side, knowing what to expect. Quickly, Cornelious turned back to his team and revealed his new plan.

Clearly, the upperclassmen were skeptical, but Rodney voiced his concerns the loudest. "Are you sure you want to risk losing to those Mainland dogs?"

"It'll work," Cornelious stared Rodney right in the eyes.

"I have never lost to Mainland in all my years on Varsity. I don't plan on changing that tonight."

"Trust me, it'll work."

"Trust? You're just a freshman....but....okay." Rodney turned back to the team huddle, "Run Gibbz's play. If we win, we win. If we lose, well you lose," Rodney threatened Cornelious, who confidently nodded back in reply.

As Rodney yelled hike, Cornelious ran wide right, caught the ball and then turned around and tossed it backwards to Jason Scott. The second the ball left Neal's hands he was tackled by three Mainland players. Hence, Jason had an easy wide-open run in for a touchdown.

The announcer boomed enthusiastically, "WWWWEEEEE DID IT!"

Of course, the crowd went wild. Chants, necessary but inappropriate, were yelled and Asbury pride burned bright. After the game, the players came out to hug their parents, and accept praises from friends and fans alike.

"Let's go over and say congrats," Carly said, as Cornelious walked out of the locker room.

"Hold on a sec. The gov'ner must see him first," Maddie joked in a fake British accent.

"You look great. I mean did great...great job cheering," Pilot told Carly blushing.

Taken back by the compliment, Carly kissed Pilot on the cheek, leaving him struggling for air.

"Uh-oh. Doesn't look good," Maddie noticed Mr. Gibbz yelling at Cornelious. "That's ridiculous, I'm gonna go save him." Maddie walked right over to Cornelious and Mr. Gibbz, overhearing some of the conversation before interrupting.

"And you honestly think, it was a good idea for you to pass up the opportunity to score the winning touchdown?"

"Dad, er, sir, it was the only way to win, sir," Cornelious said keeping his head down.

"So what? Losing is just as bad as not being the hero."

"Are you serious?"

Jeremiah Gibbz turned around and looked into the eyes of the biggest nuisance in his life---a fourteen-year-old girl. "Listen, you just march your high-tops right back to your other 'friends' and let our father-son conversation continue."

"Yeah right. You don't know how to be a father. Cornelious just won the game, and here you are yelling at him for not being selfish."

"You don't know anything girlie." Turning back to his son, "Why do you hang out with her Cornelious?"

"I...er..."

"This conversation is over with. I'll see you at home young man."

When Cornelious was sure his dad was gone, he wheeled on Maddie. "You don't have to stand up for me, I'm fine," Cornelious gathered up his bags and pushed past Maddie.

Jogging to catch up, Maddie stopped him with a hand on his forearm. "Sorry for trying to help. I just hate how he always gets on you. The only reason we won is because of you, and everyone knows it." Maddie couldn't understand why he was getting so upset. It's about time he started standing up to his dad, she thought.

"Tell that to them," Cornelious motioned to the adoring groups of girls surrounding Jason.

"Wow. I know you're not jealous of Jason Scott," Maddie crossed her arms, and arched her eyebrows.

Cornelious thought about it, and agreed. "Yeah...Sorry, he just gets me in such a bad mood."

Maddie smiled and once again told him how fantastic he played.

"So we going to the after-party?" Nya asked, as Cornelious and Maddie joined the group in the parking lot, where Nya had a car waiting to take them to Jason's.

****

When Maddie, Carly, Pilot, Cornelious, and Nya entered Jason Scott's mansion, the first thought that occurred to each of them was 'Waterslide?' Walking into the Scott's mansion, there was an open area under a huge banister that usually housed large, leather furniture, and a huge LCD flat screen TV. But tonight, there was a giant pool filled with red water (for Asbury pride), and a waterslide hanging from the upstairs banister.

"Now this is a par-tay!" Nya yelled as she ran off to join in the fun.

"You ladies want something to drink?" Ed asked as he handed a cup to Maddie and Carly.

"Er, no thanks."

"I'm good too."

"Relax, most people are drinking water," Ed shook his head, grinning.

"Oh, well sure give me some H2O," Carly said.

"Seriously, H2O? Are you sure you didn't drink anything?" Cornelious laughed as Carly glared back. The foursome made their way past their fellow classmates who were playing games, and joyously celebrating the day's undefeated record against Mainland.

"Hey Cornelious, great job today."

"You won, too?"

"Thanks Alexis and Hannah," Cornelious laughed---
Hannah was cheering and she didn't even know we won?

"So, you wanna go down the slide with me?" Alexis
asked, pulling Cornelious towards the stairs.

"Nah, I'm good. I'm just gonna chill down here."

Alexis was clearly disappointed, but shrugged it off and
grabbed her friend. "Your loss...come on Hannah."

Maddie and Carly decided to take a tour of the house, or
rather Carly made Maddie come along because she didn't
want to be alone with Jason. This left Pilot and Cornelious
ample time to stand around people-watching.

"So, I wanted to wait until our next 'meeting' but I think I
have a hunch," Pilot said.

"What?"

"Well, clearly the robber isn't rich. So, I was thinking of
possible West Asburyans with motives. And then it hit me. JB
and the Pitbulls! I mean, did you see the watches they were
wearing a few weeks ago on the boardwalk?"

"I don't know, JB is pretty dumb. He would definitely
leave a fingerprint behind. And he definitely doesn't have a
cat," Cornelious replied.

"Well, maybe he skins them! Or more likely maybe the cat
thing doesn't matter. I mean it is a stupid idea. There's no way
it's important."

"Oh really? So is it stupid because I thought of it, or
stupid because...because..." Carly sputtered as she ran out of

the house in tears.

"Should I go comfort her?" Jason asked as he watched her run out the door.

"No way. I'll go get her. I think we're leaving, now. C'mon guys." Maddie thanked Jason for the tour, who just replied with, "I always give tours to future servants." If Carly hadn't been upset, Maddie would have retorted with something clever, or possibly punched him in the face. As it was, she turned and walked out of the house.

"Hey, where are you guys going?" Eric asked when he realized Maddie was leaving and the guys were heading in the same direction.

"Sorry man, we gotta go. See ya Monday," Cornelious called. As he stepped outside Jason's house he realized what they were facing---the walk home. "This is gonna be awkward." Cornelious grumbled, pulling a speechless Pilot out of the house and down the street.

Even though Pilot must've apologized to Carly more times than supermodels look at themselves in a mirror during the course of a day, Carly wouldn't even acknowledge his existence. Cornelious and Maddie were so tired of trying to console each of them, that after dropping off Carly at her house, the trio crashed in Maddie's room.

16

Mr. McKlien entered his Honors Geometry classroom everyday wearing the same I-hate-what-my-life-has-become expression, while carrying his torn-up leather briefcase. Cornelious was more than willing to bet the contents of the case consisted of jelly donuts and coffee cakes. Whenever there was a pause in his lessons or the students were testing, Mr. McKlien would be chomping down on his various desserts. Maddie constantly asked to switch seats with Cornelious for she feared his buttons would pop off, leaving her blind for the remainder of her life. Though he was quite gluttonous, he never missed a cheat, and it was rumored his eyes were switched with a hawk's during his birth. Mr.

McKlien was also the type of teacher who handed out detention slips more often than the hourly free samples of laffy-taffy on the boardwalk. But, Cornelious mused, what made Mr. McKlien most pathetic was the fact he had been divorced four times and all of them were to mail-order brides from Tokyo.

"GIBBZ!" bellowed Mr. McKlien.

Crap, thought Cornelious, did I miss something? He gazed over to where Maddie was sitting, and almost laughed as she shielded her eyes from wherever Mr. McKlien decided to stand.

"GIBBZ, ARE YA DEAF BOY?" Mr. McKlien beckoned him to the front of the room. It wasn't until he made his way to the front that he realized his saving grace. The old man was handing him a yellow REPORT TO GUIDANCE slip. Thanking the Lord, he stepped out of the classroom and practically skipped down to the guidance room.

When he pulled open the doors, he was surprised to find Ms. Clarke waiting for him to arrive. He started to apologize for taking so long, but Ms. Clarke wouldn't hear it. She asked if it would be okay to tape record the sessions so she didn't have to write anything down this time. Cornelious saw no harm and said of course it would be fine.

After offering him a mint, she questioned him about his relationship (or lack thereof) with his parents. Then, they discussed the stress of being a governor's son and the sole heir to billions. Cornelious dejectedly explained the pressure he constantly felt from his father. "All he cares about is portraying a perfect image."

Ms. Clarke looked at him with understanding eyes. "That must be very difficult. Well, what about your relationship with your mother.?" Ms. Clarke inquired.

Cornelious told her that he sometimes felt like she valued "rich people things" more than him. "What do you mean by 'rich people things'? What are these things exactly?" Ms. Clarke questioned.

Although it was easy to talk to Ms. Clarke, Cornelious didn't want to become like Mark Spirka, the kid who visited the guidance counselor on a regular basis. Ms. Clarke was sensing that Cornelious was getting antsy and decided to finish up the session.

"You see, you aren't feeling worthless," Ms. Clarke concluded, "but rather unseen, literally and figuratively."

Cornelious was busy trying to figure out what it meant to be unseen figuratively (something he would have to ask Maddie about), when Ms. Clarke began to question him about his friends.

Cornelious revealed how they met, and Ms. Clarke listened patiently. But Cornelious wasn't entirely sure that she was listening the whole time, and his eyes kept drifting to the snow globes in the corner. Ms. Clarke possessed a plethora of snow globes, which actually all resembled each other. Instead of white snow falling, golden coins or glitter fell over tall building structures or rainbows. Cornelious figured she liked to picture herself anywhere other than Asbury in her downtime. Which he didn't blame her for, because who wants to listen to kids' problems all day?

"So... you're basically saying that you're the reason you four have managed to become friends, and you feel responsible for whether or not you four remain that way." Ms. Clarke leaned all the way forward, as if she discovered a new fact and wanted to make sure Cornelious heard her correctly.

"Um, not exactly, no." By this point Cornelious was wondering whether he should act like he had to go to the bathroom, or perhaps fake a seizure.

"You don't see it yet, but you will. Trust me," then she added rather quietly, "have you ever tried to make new friends?"

"Have you been talking to my dad?" Cornelious asked suspiciously.

"No... Have you?" Ms. Clarke retorted.

"Not really, no."

"Do you think it's because of the time you spend with Pilot, Carly, and Maddie?"

Cornelious was beginning to think this conversation was taking the form of an endless circle, when Ms. Clarke stood up and said her nine o'clock was here, and that she was looking forward to their next 'get-together.'

****

"Hey guys, I've got some big news," Pilot smiled.

"What, you hit puberty?" Maddie asked, and Cornelious laughed.

"No," scowled Pilot, then he quickly added, "I mean, yes!

But that's not what I'm talking about!" Pilot pleaded helplessly, which made Cornelious and Maddie explode into even more laughter.

However, they stopped immediately when Carly gave them her death-stare.

"Maybe I should just tell Carly. Even though it pertains to the case. Directly."

"Okay, okay. Spill," Maddie said, unraveling her peanut butter and jelly sandwich from its foil wrappings.

"Well, I found some pretty interesting evidence from the Wallabee break-in. Apparently there were some strands of cat hair present throughout the crime scene, which baffles the cops seeing as Mrs. Wallabee is allergic to them! Which would also mean---

"That I was right about the importance of the cat hairs!" Carly squealed, and glared at Pilot.

"I don't know how many times I have to say sorry and that I was wrong. I'll never doubt you again," Pilot pleaded.

"Well, seeing as I was right...and I don't like to hold grudges...I'll accept your apology." Carly sat up straighter and pushed her hair back, ensuring everyone knew she was right all along.

"YES! I mean, thank you," Pilot beamed at Carly, who tried to hide her smile.

"Okay, now that everything is good in la-la land can we get back to the case at hand?" Maddie asked.

With everyone nodding in assent, Pilot continued, "And we can finally establish an important link between both break-ins!"

"Wait a sec... how did the papers not get a hold of this?" Cornelious inquired.

"The police wanted to keep it low key. Ya know, in case the robber is in this for the fame," Pilot stated, taking a bite of his soggy tuna sandwich, which he almost immediately spit out.

"But I thought it was pretty obvious the thief doesn't care about fame. He doesn't even leave an obvious trace or have a pattern," Carly stated, offering Pilot some of her lunch.

"We don't know if he has a pattern yet. Seeing as this is only his second theft," Pilot remarked, biting into an apple.

"Which means that we're going to have to start looking for any possible pattern," Maddie stated.

"If there's another break-in," Cornelious added.

"Of course, there's going to be another one. I think the perp's just getting warmed up," Maddie countered.

"But, how'd you find out all this information?" Carly wondered all of a sudden.

"Well, I figured it would be best if we knew what the police were thinking so we could have their information, as well as ours. So I hacked into their mainframe, and have kept it open and running ever since," Pilot said nonchalantly.

"That really is quite impressive," Carly smiled, and Pilot turned pinker than a fresh salmon.

17

"Do re mi fa so la team tryouts are scheduled for the Monday after Thanksgiving breakkk if you wish to be on our famous debate team! And a big CONGRATULATIONS goes out to the girls' soccer team and boy's football team for winning seasons! Oh yeah! Asbury High was fortunate to have both teams head to the state semi-finals. That touchdown is still debatable boys... Anywho-who, congrats again! As for the graffiti on the..." sang Ms. Dugan. Although most students looked forward to Ms. Dugan singing the news over the loudspeaker each morning--- yes singing, because she happens to be an ex-Broadway superstar---the students were surprised the announcements were being read, or rather sang, during sixth period.

"I was wondering why we didn't hear any announcements

this morning," Peetie murmured to Maddie.

"They were probably flustered or something," Maddie guessed.

"Well, I heard someone wrapped Coste's car in cellophane," Jazz added.

"Classic. I wish we thought of that last year when the teachers didn't really care," Cornelious laughed, although Jazz turned away from the conversation when Cornelious joined.

When the announcements finally wrapped up, Mr. Caulfield took control of his classroom again. Mr. Caulfield was very interesting, very funny, and very handsome. Three traits that were essential for teaching any history class, let alone a bunch of freshmen. Because Mr. Caulfield was always seen wearing a bowtie, many reported seeing him sunbathing in bowties of various colors and styles in the summer. However, the one trait that separates Mr. Caulfield from about ninety percent of the teachers in Asbury High is where he resides...in West Asbury. With the handsome paycheck each teacher receives, most live in condos or houses in East Asbury. Nevertheless, each student loved Mr. Caulfield--- especially when he brought in his homemade candies. In fact, his candies became so famous in Asbury, that on weekends in the summer Mr. Caulfield sold them on the boardwalk, and at very cheap prices.

"Many say that what doesn't kill you, makes you stronger. Now, I believe the soccer and football players in this classroom---whom have suffered recent losses---may attest to that idea," Mr. Caulfield paused for dramatic effect as he pulled down a map of the world circa 1930. "I think that Germany in the 1930's would also support that idea. Coming off of a loss in WWI, and faced with humiliating reparations, Germany needed a something or someone to piece them back together. Unfortunately..."

****

"Man oh man, do I love Gym," Maddie laughed as she headed up the stairs with Cornelious to Biology.

"You're just happy cuz you got to throw the dodgeball right into Jason's face."

"True. But I wish I could've gotten Ed too. Two birds with one stone and all."

When Cornelious and Maddie entered Biology, it was clear something major had just taken place. With a substitute in the room, the class should've been chaotic or at least mischievous, but instead an eerie silence resounded throughout the room.

"Who died?" Cornelious whispered to Maddie.

"Let's just take our seats," Maddie replied, sliding into her seat.

"I mean, it does make sense. Except, well, you'd think she'd be dressing better now," Alexis sneered, looking Maddie over.

"Are you...is she talking to me?... Now I'm confused," Maddie turned to Cornelious, who shrugged and began digging his notebook out of his bag.

"Obviously she's talking to you. I knew the thief would be a woman. I just knew it! Men... we get blamed for everything," Ed boasted.

"What?! I didn't steal anything," Maddie stated incredulously.

The class anxiously turned in their stools to watch the showdown between the two, awaiting one of the most-anticipated events in high school: the fight. Although fights may only take place three or four times each year, when they occurred everyone knew. Some kids claimed to possess an uncanny ability to sense a fight, minutes before it began. Nowadays, the best teachers had to possess this intuition and also be qualified to break up fights. Largely because whenever a fight broke out, everyone seemed to digress back to the gladiator days, forming a circle and calling for blood.

"I thought you were supposed to be smart, Mad-e-line. I never said you in particular, did I?"

Cornelious grabbed Maddie before she could jump from her stool and gauge out Ed's eyes. "Ed, seriously. Cut to the chase. What or who are you talking about?"

"Neal, Neal... oh, you must not have heard. Apparently, Mrs. Petrozza was brought in for questioning a few hours ago...as the prime suspect...in the recent robberies," Ed beamed, as if he just won the lottery.

"Is that it? You guys are morons, that doesn't mean anything. Maybe she's a witness, or something...How'd you find out anyway?" Cornelious questioned, still gripping Maddie, who had turned pale and stopped trying to wriggle loose.

"Maria Scott is the receptionist at the police department,

so she called Jason after Gym," Alexis interjected.

"And he just thought it was, what? His job to tell the whole school?!" Maddie angrily asked.

"I mean someone had to. But hey if you need some extra money when your mom's in jail, I'll put in a good word for you with my parents," laughed Ed, as he got up from his stool and started walking over to Maddie.

"Shut up, dude," Cornelious warned.

"Or if you need somewhere to live when your house gets repoed, my house is always free," Ed continued to laugh as he stopped walking, and stood right in front of Maddie.

"Seriously, Ed. I'm warning you."

"Or if you just need someone to lean on, I---umpf."

Although the class was nervously awaiting a fight, no one expected Cornelious to push Maddie aside, lunge out of his chair, and punch Ed in the face.

"OOOWWWWWW!IFINKEWBROJEMENOSE!" yelled Ed, as he unsuccessfully tried to hold the blood from pouring out of his nose.

"Whoa! What just happened?" the substitute spun around from writing pointless directions on the board. "I am not qualified for this. I am NOT qualified for this. Oh my gosh! I was just supposed to write some stuff down, and then act like I care. Ummm. Go to the principal. Both of you...Please?"

Knowing that disagreeing would be pointless, and kind of feeling bad for the rookie sub, the boys walked out the door and headed to Coste's.

Once in Coste's office, the boys knew better than to take a

seat. Principal Coste had his faithful bluetooth plugged in, and upon stepping into his office, the boys glanced at each other, regretting the fight immediately. After all, they did just suffer through three years of Coste's wrath in Middle School. When the bald man turned around and unplugged, Cornelious studied his Principal, yet again. With boyish features and a medium build, parents simply did not believe their children when they voiced their discomfort and displeasure towards Mr. Coste. However, Mr. Coste was the type of person who became a Principal to ensure each child felt as miserable as he always did. Whether it was doling out extreme and unnecessary punishments (Carly and Pilot once had to find and collect ten pieces---each---of already-chewed chewing gum from the blacktop, under supervision---which took four hours!), or berating his pupils in public, Mr. Coste was glad to be of service. What was even worse for the students in Asbury was Mr. Coste's ability to manipulate parents, fellow teachers, and even the school system. Hence, complaints about Mr. Coste fell on deaf ears. Although students feared the consequences, everyone still enjoyed messing with him.

"You boys thought it would be a good idea to fight with a new sub in town, eh?" Mr. Coste smirked as he stared both boys in the eyes, at the same time.

"Well...er...uh...I," Cornelious began.

"EBROKEMENOSENDATSYUMBLEEDIN," mumbled Ed, still holding his nose.

"Hold on! If yer bleedin' GET OUT OF MY OFFICE!"

bellowed Mr Coste, as Ed scrambled out the door and down the hall to the nurse's. "This is a new office, and I will not have it stained with blood!"

"Yet," Cornelious mumbled.

"What was that, boy?" Mr. Coste turned his attention to Cornelious. "Ahh, Mr. Gibbz. I wondered when I'd be seeing you or your little friends in my office. Believe me when I say, I've been looking forward to it." Mr. Coste smiled a devilish grin and drummed his fingers patiently on his desk.

"Oh, uh...yeah. Me too."

Before Cornelious knew it, Coste sprung up from behind his desk, and pulled Cornelious close to his face. "Listen, smart-alec. If it was up to me, you would have Saturday detentions for the next month. But I also know it's almost basketball season and your generous father would be displeased if you missed some games."

Cornelious was speechless, for once he'd have to thank his father for something.

"However, this deed cannot go completely unpunished. What example would I be setting in my new post?"

Nevermind that thanks dad, Cornelious thought. But Coste had released him and was now strolling around his office. Cornelious had the feeling Coste was speaking more to himself than Cornelious now.

"Therefore, you have two choices. The first option is volunteering in West Asbury---something could be arranged. Or you can give a speech at our next assembly on the importance of nonviolence in school." Cornelious could see the gleam in Coste's eyes, and knew that Coste had been thinking of new punishments to try out.

"I'll do the school speech," Cornelious volunteered, knowing Coste would choose the opposite of what Cornelious wished.

"Okay, I guess it's settled...ahh wait, I'm sorry. The next assembly is a pep rally, and we're not giving an informational assembly until May. I guess you'll just have to volunteer. I'll need you to get some signatures signifying forty hours of volunteering. Don't worry you'll have plenty of time, let's say a month?"

"Er, thank you Principal Coste," Cornelious began backing out of the office.

"And I don't want to see you in this office again!" roared Principal Coste.

18

"Brrrrrr, I thought these games were over," Carly complained as she wrapped her jacket tighter around herself.

"They are. This is the Thanksgiving morning alumni game," Pilot explained as he sat down with a tray containing three steamy mugs of hot cocoa, courtesy of Ms. Owens.

"Which basically means it's a chance for TJ Scott and Jeremiah Gibbz, and all the rest of the dads living in the past, to try to prove themselves worthy," added Maddie.

Unfortunately for the current members of the Asbury High football team, Maddie was correct. The Asbury High alumni football game is one of the most anticipated events of the fall, and ambulances know to standby. In fact, last year six ambulances were needed to carry back injured players, after their fathers got 'too rough.'

"I just hope Cornelious doesn't get hurt. Basketball tryouts are tomorrow," Maddie anxiously stated, gulping down Ms. Owen's hot cocoa.

"I always thought that was rough. I mean the day after Thanksgiving? Thank gosh our cheerleading tryouts are way before any major food holidays."

Before Maddie or Pilot could respond, the rest of the bleachers filled up and the three were squished together. Maddie couldn't help but notice the smile on both Pilot's and Carly's faces.

Overall, the game was rough. Fathers and sons dueled until the end, and even after the game was called some fathers were pleading for more time. This year only two ambulances were needed, and thankfully Cornelious was not in any of them.

"Thanks for coming guys," Cornelious told the gang after the game.

"Anytime, we love seeing you bring down your dad," Pilot stated.

"Well, Mr. Owens. I'm happy to know you take pleasure in my pain," Mr. Gibbz appeared out of nowhere, looking angrier than a nest of hornets.

"Don't worry, sir. He's not the only one," Maddie smiled.

"Hmph. It's time to go Cornelious, Dane's airplane has just arrived."

****

People love various holidays for different reasons. Maddie loved Christmas because of the snow and the cookies. Cornelious loved the Fourth of July, for the fireworks and the weather. Carly loved Easter due to the pretty colors and Reese's eggs (genius idea, by the way). And Pilot loved Thanksgiving, but it was not because of the delicious and never-ending food. Nor was it the fact that the historical origins of this marvelous holiday amused him. But the real reason for his love of Thanksgiving, is that Pilot and his mother spent every Thanksgiving with the Petrozzas. Thanksgiving with the Petrozzas was always priceless, and memorable to say the least. Especially when Maddie's grandmother La was in town.

Even though Mrs. Petrozza may be a person of interest in the Asbury thefts, she made sure Thanksgiving continued as usual. The long wooden table was brought in from the auto shop and cleaned thoroughly. Ms. Owens made sure to bring over her homemade Thanksgiving tablecloth, consisting of fifty squares, which depicted a varying plate of turkey dinner in each state. Trent and Alec made their annual remote truce, which allowed Sophia to finally control the TV, as she tuned into the repeats of televised parades. The twins were busy running around the kitchen stirring, chopping, and secretly adding hot sauce to various items (this fact was not discovered until years later, when someone finally mentioned the spicy quality of the mashed potatoes). Maddie relaxed and hung out with her dad and Pilot, and breathed in the delicious fumes of the turkey day celebrations. As the night wore on everyone forgot about the recent troubles and dug into the tantalizing turkey and magnificent meal. After many stories were told, and the food was pretty much destroyed, the Petrozzas and the Owens all sat around waiting for dessert.

"Can we have dessert now?" pleaded Daniel.

"Yeah, can we? Can we?" Shannon begged.

But before anyone could volunteer to bring in the desert, La piped up. "No dessert for me! No thanks."

Maddie was utterly surprised. "But La you love dessert. You usually live for it."

"Yeah, mom, are you feeling okay?"

"Yes. Yes, I'm fine. Remember just last weekend I was alligator-wrestling down in New Orleans?"

"Of course. Those pictures were, er, timeless." Mr. Petrozza assured his mother. "But why won't you have a little morsel of dessert. Pilot even made, er, something this year."

Something was a good description. Pilot had tried to make pudding, but ending up making a silver liquidy thing that made him think that the Fantastic Four's Silver Surfer had sprung a leak.

"Oh alright, alright. If you must know I ate a cookie on the living room table earlier and honestly, it didn't taste good. At all. I'm sorry."

Almost immediately Maddie began bursting into a laughing fit, and when she tried to explain to everyone why, tears trickled out of her eyes. Realizing she was on the verge of hysteria, she ran into the living room, and came back with a tanish circle in her hand. "Th--th--this isn't a--a--a cookie...it's---it's---it's--a--- a CANDLE!"

It took a second for everyone to register that La had not consumed a cookie, but rather a candle. After that it was impossible to keep a straight face for the rest of the evening.

****

Across town, Cornelious found himself wishing it was the Fourth of July. At least that's a holiday away from my parents, he thought to himself. Only for the major holidays would one find the Gibbz family sitting in the million-dollar-dining-room or enjoying a meal together. Having the meal brought in by caterers, one piece at a time (turkey first, then mashed potatoes, followed by green bean casserole, etc), and placed on the lavish italian-styled glass table, underneath the extensive glass regency model chandelier, made for a picture-perfect meal. Exactly as Jeremiah Gibbz intended.

"Hey Cornelious, could you pass the cranberry sauce?"

"Yeah, here Dane." Cornelious passed the disgusting red mold to his cousin, making sure there was enough food in his mouth so he would have a reason not to engage in conversation with his father. Cornelious took this time to look over his cousin, and think about how his father probably wished they were switched at birth or something. Although Dane resembled Cornelious in some ways, similar build and eyes, his curly black hair and pale skin set him apart from the rest of the Gibbz clan. However, his desire to follow in Jeremiah Gibbz' footsteps allowed Jeremiah to gladly invite him over for most major holidays and summer vacations. Cornelious didn't really mind; he actually enjoyed having

Dane stay over, and take some of the pressure off of him.

"Honey, did you make sure there were enough leftovers for Howie?"

"Nancy, I told you. Howie's food accommodations are well taken care of," Mr. Gibbz replied. "Cornelious did you make sure to---"

Cornelious never found out what his father was about to say, for at that very moment a reporter leapt out from the wicker closet, and rolled right next to the table between Cornelious and Jeremiah. Unfortunately, the reporter was able to take some quick shots of the family choking on their food in surprise.

"Well, I'll be! A photo op! Yippeee!" Nancy Gibbz squealed in delight, and sat up straighter, flashing her supermodel smile.

Shrugging off her excitement, the reporter quickly asked in a fast-paced, slightly southern accent---which made Cornelious think of the fast-talking gangsters of the twenties they had learned about last year---"How does it feel to be the number one richest family in Asbury, as proclaimed in the latest 'Fortune Fine 25' rankings, yet again? Scared you may be a target of the next theft?"

The reporter continued to rattle off questions, so Dane and Cornelious excused themselves and took the elevator to Cornelious' room. After a Thanksgiving at the Gibbz's, taking the winding staircase to the top floor was a task too daunting for anyone.

19

Brandan and Dennis know the last thing customers want two days after Thanksgiving is turkey, or any aspect of turkey day leftovers. However, they also know many people desire something sweet. Therefore, the release of Brady's Tacos and Pancakes dessert menu not only provides sweetness, but also signals the upcoming holiday season for each Asburyan.

"And here are the Cookie Tacos, for some very hungry customers." Ms. Owens dropped off four orders of chocolate ice-cream drizzled with marshmallows, sprinkled in nuts, and wrapped in warm cookie dough shell---otherwise known as the Cookie Taco---just as an exhausted Cornelious took his place beside Maddie in the gang's usual worn-in corner booth. Luckily for Pilot, she couldn't stay to chat because Brady's was very busy this time of year.

"How were tryouts?" Carly inquired.

"Ever hear of 10-8-6-4-2s? We have to run up and back ten times, then eight times, then six, then four, then two, and then someone has to make a foul shot to end it. It's Baruff's idea of how to get in sprint shape, and its deadly," Cornelious explained, exhausted. "But what about your tryouts Mads? You guys are lucky you didn't have two-a-days."

"Well, that's probably because not too many girls tried out, so Nya and I got moved up to Varsity. Willy is pretty laid back, so I don't think this season will be too hard. Nya is definitely going to start, I'm thinking sixth man for me…hopefully."

"Nice. Congrats. Baruff seems like a great coach, I can tell. He does have the tendency to use Italian words or use, er, unintelligent phrases. But it keeps us laughing, which is good."

Pilot, who was just about done his Cookie Taco and wanted to steer the conversation away from sports, asked if anything special happened on Turkey Day, and then told the story of La's cookie. After finishing the remaining dessert, Cornelious remembered the reporter who was hiding in the wicker closet and told everyone his version. His retelling was pretty accurate, except that he added that the reporter accidentally knocked his dad over and landed on Howie.

"Well, at least you guys had an enjoyable Thanksgiving. Mom and Dad made us drive to Aunt Deedee's and everyone insisted on pinching my cheeks and treating me a like a child. And asking me to do various cheers for them. Gosh, it was so embarrassing. Seriously guys! Stop laughing..." But even Carly had to laugh, because the gang knew she was always one to step into the limelight and enjoy an audience.

****

The next morning was a typical Sunday morning in Asbury. Lawns were mowed, by landscapers in the East and fathers in the West, and most families were enjoying a typical Sunday morning pancake breakfast. The student-athletes, musicians, and academics were enjoying a much-needed day off from practice, meetings, and study sessions. Everyone in Asbury was relaxing---except for a group of twenty in Asbury's only library (on the West Side). Although each member of this group would've preferred eating pancakes, laying around, or even mowing lawns, they found themselves sitting in a circle, on the uncomfortable gray and blue cut-pile carpet, listening to a lady wearing an "I love horses, and they nose it!" sweater---with the horse's nose nuzzling the neck of the sweater.

"Now, ladies and gentlemen, I need your opinions. 'The Westing Game' is a tale that constantly makes you reconsider and often doubt each character, as well as yourself. Who agrees?"

"Well, certainly I agree. I especially loved the stock market aspect of the book. It's quite rare in books these days," added a squirrel-like boy who was a year older than Maddie, but looked about five years younger.

"Good observation Milton. Anyone else? Hmmm, Madeline, what about you?"

Although Maddie loved reading and really enjoyed school, she always hated when teachers singled her out for questioning. Especially when it was Ms. Cunningham, for she had a tendency to come right over to where you were sitting and bend down until your noses almost touched. Edging back a little, Maddie explained that her favorite part was that she was totally blind-sided by who the bomber was in the end! She wholeheartedly believed it was anyone other than that person.

At this comment, Alexis Johnson snorted, "I knew the whole time."

However, Ms. Cunningham disregarded Alexis and smiled, "What we have here is the Red Herring effect. Sometimes we get so drawn into believing one person is guilty---and this usually is the person who seems the most guilty---that we lose sight of the real perpetrator. But don't forget that we must always ask ourselves the most dangerous question in the world...why? Why? What is the motive?"

After a few more pointless comments, Ms. Cunningham begrudgingly let the group go and assigned a new book for them to 'digest.'

"Whew, I thought we'd never get out of there," Peetie laughed, leaving the library and heading back home.

"I know. It's brutal in there," Maddie wholeheartedly answered.

"Hey guys, wait up!"

Maddie and Peetie turned around and waited for Milton to scurry towards them so they could walk back home together.

"That book completely enthralled me. I was writing down motives and suspects the whole time. Wow!" Milton brought out two notebooks worth of work. "Hey, if you want to get together and read the next book, I could get you your own notebook. It could be fun!" Milton was staring intently at Maddie.

Peetie looked over at Maddie and tried hard not to laugh. "Aw Milton, I would but I have basketball, and school, and a lot going on. I usually read the books on bus rides to and from games," Maddie began, but seeing how heartbroken Milton appeared she added, "But maybe we can get together in study hall and compare notes or something."

"Really?! I'd love that! Well, see ya later!"

Maddie and Peetie kept walking down the road until they got to the junkyard, at which Maddie turned left and Peetie headed right towards the old Hartman Hotel (where she lives).

"See ya tomorrow...oh, unless you're too busy with Milton," Peetie smiled.

"Ugh, he only likes me because no other girls talk to him...it's kind of sad," Maddie replied.

"Yeah, yeah. But you and Milton would make a great couple!" Peetie laughed as she turned and headed home.

Cunningham would just love that, Maddie thought. She'd probably insist on a wedding in the library. Maddie walked into her kitchen and wasn't surprised to see Cornelious and Pilot hanging on every word Trent spoke. Sighing, she grabbed some milk and poured herself a tall glass.

"And girls always say something different than what they want. And they never tell you what they're really thinking," the expert told his eager listeners. Maddie considered this new piece of information, and laughed.

"What's so funny about that? It's true. I bet if I asked you to tell us what you're thinking right now, you wouldn't," Trent added smugly.

"You don't have to, though," Pilot hated being in between brother-sister fights, especially at the Petrozza's.

Maddie smiled and walked around them to the staircase, "If you want to know so badly, I'll tell you. I'm picturing myself marrying Milton Davies in a luxurious library wedding ceremony."

All three guys sat there with their mouths open and couldn't believe their ears.

"What?" Pilot gasped.

"Are you serious? What's so special about Milton Davies? He looks like a squirrel," Cornelious quickly countered.

"I don't know...he's a nice guy. What? Are you jealous?"

"No. It's--"

"Don't listen to her man. That's my point exactly, women love to make up stories," Trent concluded as he got up and went into the next room to fight Alec for the remote.

Maddie decided to drop it, because it was useless to explain why she was picturing herself marrying Milton. Besides they had bigger things to discuss.

"Why are you guys here anyway? Is there a break in the case?"

"No."

"I wish. But I had to come over to get your dad to sign my volunteer service papers for Coste."

"Sounds fun," Maddie took a seat at the kitchen table and joined her friends.

"Loads. So... How was book club?" Cornelious asked, still wondering why Maddie was picturing herself marrying Milton.

"Pointless...actually, I did learn something."

"Yippe!" Pilot exclaimed.

Ignoring Pilot, Maddie continued, "It's about the case...To find the thief we must determine his motive."

20

Asbury citizens may not agree on many matters, the distribution of funds and special treatment of some being just the tip of the iceberg. However, when it came to the Asbury Aces (high school sports teams), you could bet your Aunt Suzy everyone came together for support. Naturally, some parents argued over playing time and players' abilities. Nevertheless, the Aces helped to unify Asbury---if only for one to two hours at a time.

With this knowledge in mind, student-athletes often felt pressured to perform. The fact that the first basketball game of the season was at home, and a double-header, left a handful of players feeling queasy throughout the day. Maddie and Cornelious, however, were happy to be on Varsity and couldn't be more excited. The girl's team was scheduled for five o'clock, and the boys were to play right after. This schedule left plenty of time for Maddie and Cornelious to work on Moskow's newest essay assignment (which included drawing the introduction paragraph instead of writing it), in the library. Cornelious was attempting to justify why his first paragraph resembled a giant pizza, when Pilot burst into the library, dragging Carly behind him.

"What the---" Maddie began.

"I had to tell you guys," Pilot started.

"Before their games though?" Carly questioned clearly annoyed but still holding hands with Pilot.

"Especially before their games," Pilot glanced around the library and lowered his voice. "There's been another break-in, at the Tibbits'."

"No way! I thought they just updated their security," Cornelious replied.

"Are you one hundred percent positive, Pilot?" Maddie replied, thinking deeply.

"Of course. I have the police station's computer running live and sending me updates on the case directly to my phone."

"Impressive," Carly genuinely smiled, at which point Pilot realized they were still holding hands and released his grip.

"Crap! I can't be thinking about this now! I have a game in two hours," Maddie muttered.

"I thought you'd want to know," Pilot said crestfallen.

Feeling bad, Maddie assured Pilot that it was better he told them any news right away, as it would allow them to see if anyone was acting suspicious, for the police were keeping any new developments and break-ins under wraps. The gang decided that after the double-header they would head back to Maddie's to rewrite the facts and try to investigate the newest crime scene as soon as possible.

****

"Man oh man! I cannot believe our first game is over. Just like that! Did you see that sweet block I had in the third?" Nya was pantomiming her glorious block as the two left the locker room and rejoined reality.

"You know Nya, I thought you were going to break her nose."

"Well, Madeline sometimes that's the only way to win."

"We won by 30."

"Nuh uh. We only won by 29," Nya smiled as she walked away and joined her admirers (over-zealous family members) in the bleachers. After a few minutes of thanking people for coming and accepting congratulations from random people, Maddie made her way over to where Pilot was sitting. Leave it to Pilot to be fiddling with some electronic device at a basketball game, Maddie thought.

"Hey Pi, some game, eh?" Maddie sat next to him, and looked to see what he was doing.

"You did great...from what I could guess, I mean. I thought you said you weren't, er, beginning?"

"You mean starting?"

"Yeah, that's it. But anyway, I watched half the game. But when you guys were up by 18, I lost interest."

"As did I."

Their conversation was cut short as the guy's team jogged into the gymnasium, followed by the cheerleaders. Maddie and Pilot spent a few moments whooping and cheering for Carly and Cornelious. Halfway through warm-ups, Pilot tugged on Maddie's arm and pointed towards the exit door behind the opposing fans' bleachers. Maddie was about to question Pilot, when she realized JB was acting more shady than usual, and appeared to be gathering his cronies and motioning them to follow him. Maddie and Pilot looked at each other and made an unspoken agreement to follow the Pitbulls.

Once they were outside, Maddie was glad she had put her sweats on over her uniform, and decided to wear a hat that day. Apparently, winter had decided to come early and come angry. It wasn't snowing yet, but one didn't have to be Nostradamus to predict snow would fall in a few short days.

"What if they see us?" Pilot whispered as they made their way to the boardwalk, tailing the Pitbulls at a safe distance.

"They're too obnoxious to notice anything but themselves," whispered Maddie. "And they honestly don't even do that. Have you ever sat next to one of them in class, or on the bus? They smell like two-week old veggie lasagna."

"Eww! How do you know what that smells like?"

"Once, Daniel put it in the stove, and for weeks we could NOT for the life of us figure----"

Maddie cut herself short as she pulled Pilot down beside her, in front of the cinema.

"Okay. We haven't been followed or nothin' JB. Let's go," rasped one of the Pitbulls.

From their vantage point, Maddie and Pilot watched as JB pulled up a boardwalk plank and waited until each member was successfully below before joining them himself. Hastily, Maddie and Pilot crept over to the plank, and lingered a moment before shadowing the group below. When they had both climbed under the boardwalk, and followed the gang to where Maddie decided was the area underneath the movie theater, they heard the Pitbulls speak. Unfortunately, neither Pilot nor Maddie heard any mention of thefts, nor did the Pitbulls mention East Asbury at all. Maddie and Pilot did get a full view of the Pitbull's 'residence' though. Seeing as they chose to reign supreme under the boardwalk, the area had a distinct funnel cake and seaweed smell. And, although the beach was clearly the foundation of their home, there seemed to be more cigarettes and junk food wrappers than grains of sand. Each member sat on a black chair facing JB, who ruled sprawled out on a red sofa that rested on a small platform. Furthermore, Maddie and Pilot saw boxes strewn about the area, and one appeared to be full of jewelry. Knowing it would be stupid to talk to one another, Maddie and Pilot carefully made their way back to the boardwalk.

Only after they were completely off the boardwalk and halfway to the police station, did they dare to talk to each other.

"Did you see the jewelry?"

"It had to be them! And we can lead the police right to

them!"

"This will definitely clear my mom!"

Feeling triumphant, the duo waltzed into the police station and demanded that Maria let them into the police quarters, so they can give a full statement and provide the cops with details.

Maria, who was almost done her shift, decided this was the most amusing thing that had happened all day and called in Officers Swanson and Tennett. When the two officers made their way to the waiting room where Maddie and Pilot were waiting, Maddie considered how very little these two resembled policemen. Officer Tennett was clearly the tallest man in the room (any room for that matter), and was just as skinny as he was tall. Officer Swanson was shorter than Frodo and rounder than a beach ball. Nevertheless, Maddie patiently told the officers their story. Four times.

"Shouldn't you be writing this down?" Pilot asked.

"Now that's the smartest thing you've said all night, kid," Officer Swanson grumbled.

Maddie realized these two had no intention of filing any report or making any phone calls, other than to order Chinese food. "You don't believe us, do you?"

"It's not that we don't. It's just... we just expected you two to roll up in the Mystery Machine accompanied by a talking dog who would better explain the situation to us."

Apparently, Maria, Tennett, and Swanson thought this was the joke of the century and laughed for a full minute--- which is a very long time if you're the butt of the joke.

"Oh. I didn't realize you two took all your professional cues from Scooby-Doo. We'll just let you go back to eating donuts," Maddie sweetly replied.

Officers Tennett and Swanson were so surprised by this statement that for a moment no one said anything. That is until Swanson said, "Did you just knowingly insult two men of the law?"

Pilot could tell that tonight was going to be a long night. If looks could kill Officer Tennett would have murdered Maddie, twice. Before either officer could make a move, Cornelious and Carly burst through the station doors. Cornelious walked right up to the officers and took control of the situation, beckoning them to his side and whispering to them for about five minutes. After their hushed conversation the officers told Maria to assist them out of the station, and the two walked back to their desks. Being the governor's son and richest teenager in Asbury certainly has its perks.

When the gang walked out of the station Carly rushed over to embrace both Pilot and Maddie. She quickly explained, "Well, Maria was texting Jason after the game about the 'hilarious' situation involving you two, and that the officers were 'growing impatient'. Cornelious asked if you two were still at the station, and when Jason said you were, well, we rushed over to help."

Maddie walked over to thank Cornelious, but he looked past the gang, jumped into his limo, and drove away.

21

"AND THEN...." boomed an obnoxious voice from behind Maddie, Carly, Cornelious, and Pilot in the cafeteria, "they pleaded, literally pleaded, with the cops to arrest the Pitbulls right then and there. With no evidence whatsoever."

"I always knew they were crazy," Alexis added, as the group laughed in agreement.

"Just ignore Jason. And the rest of them. His sister's a blabbermouth, I mean you knew she would tell him. Not to be mean, but it's true." Try as she might, Carly was failing in her attempt to make her friends feel better. "And at least you didn't get arrested."

Maddie was too angry to smile. She had hated being treated like a kid at the police station, and was still upset that no one believed her. To make matters worse, Maria Scott had told her brother every detail, which he happily relayed back to the entire school. Furthermore, JB and the Pitbulls now realized Pilot and Maddie had not only suspected them of theft, but had discovered their lair as well. Things were not looking good.

"Well, you brought it on yourselves," Cornelious muttered.

"Seriously? You too?"

"Yes, Maddie. Me too. It was incredibly stupid of you to follow them! For Pete's sake they're delinquents, you guys could have gotten hurt."

"I could take care of myself."

"What about Pilot? What about lack of evidence? Alibis? Motive? You can't just tell the cops to arrest someone without all of the details."

"Okay, okay. Jeesh, I get it. But you didn't see the boxes of jewelry."

"And whose fault is that? If you just waited until after my game---"

"Is that what this is about? Listen, I'm sorry I missed your game! But my mom is a prime suspect or person of interest or whatever!"

"Guys! Stop fighting!" Carly yelled.

"Yes. Leave the fighting to us." The gang looked up to see JB and a few Pitbulls standing next to their table, cracking their knuckles.

"Just leave us alone," Maddie grumbled.

"A few days ago, I may have listened. But I heard you followed us and tried to have us thrown in jail. Now that's not very nice, is it?" JB smiled.

"Shut it JB. We know you're not the town thief. Plus Jason is lying. His gossip-loving sister can talk a paper-cut victim into becoming an amputee," Cornelious replied.

After considering this for a moment, JB reached down and grabbed Pilot's sandwich, swallowing it in one bite. "You might be right, Gibbzy, but now I know to keep an eye out for you guys."

Waiting until they were out of earshot Cornelious added, "See, you pissed off JB."

"I pissed him off years ago. Didn't you hear that's how I met him."

The gang smiled, and the tension melted away as they recalled that fateful day in the second grade.

****

Following in the tradition of hosting holiday parties, Jeremiah Gibbz had been eagerly anticipating throwing this year's Christmas party. If the people of Asbury were impressed by the Halloween Ball at Pecunia Palace, then they were sure to be blown away by the Christmas party at the Gibbz mansion.

Every year, Nancy Gibbz took the phrase 'deck the halls' to a new level. The walkway leading up to the front door was lined with thousands of gumdrops, and the fountain water was replaced with eggnog---yes, eggnog. The front door was replaced with a tunnel-like entryway, made to resemble a giant present. Every variation of holiday food was placed in the dining room, and standing in there for ten seconds was sure to make you salivate. Of course, the majority of the time was spent out back where a giant pavilion was erected and surrounded with larger-than-life replicas of beloved Christmas characters. The expansive dance floor was made of green and red marble, and fake snow fell the entire time in the area beyond the pavilion.

Perhaps the best thing about the Christmas party was that the entire town was excited to join in the festivities. Unlike the Halloween Ball, where the rich reigned supreme in high-quality costumes and snubbed the West-siders for attending, the Christmas party welcomed everyone. Maybe everyone was in the holiday spirit, or maybe it was that each guest had to bring a present for randomized pollyanna at the end of the night (the rich considered it an honor to buy a gift for the less fortunate, whereas the 'less fortunate' enjoyed reaping in the goods). Needless to say, this was the one night a year in which everyone was in enjoyment at the Gibbz mansion.

Well, almost everyone. Earlier in the week, Pilot had accidentally made a dumb blonde comment which infuriated Carly. Unfortunately, before she could yell at Pilot, Jason had meandered over and asked to 'escort' Carly to the Christmas party. Knowing this would anger Pilot (and hopefully enable him to gather enough courage to make a move), she agreed. At first, Maddie shared Carly's mindset that this may enrage Pilot enough to make a move. However, now that Maddie was at the party (as a server, yes), she was finding a moping Pilot very annoying.

"You know Christmas is my favorite holiday, right?"

"Ugh, yeah." Pilot responded, stacking cups on various trays.

"Well, you didn't have to come early with me and ruin my mood. I'm getting paid good money for this, and I love these decorations.... anyway, when Carly gets here, ask her to dance."

"But I'm not her date."

"And just what does that matter? If she wants to dance with you, she will. And I'm pretty sure she will."

Pilot mulled this over and grew anxious as the guests started to arrive. Just when Maddie was about to ask Pilot to pass the snowflake cups, Carly and Jason walked under the pavilion. Although she hated to admit it, they did make a good-looking couple. Carly had her long blonde hair tied back in a loose bun, and wore a sparkly blue dress slit halfway up her left leg, stopping at the knee. Jason made sure to groom his mohawk, and wore a simple black and white tux with a blue bow-tie to match Carly. Maddie was about to wave, but stopped when she realized Pilot had already beckoned them over.

"Driver, my main man," Jason slapped Pilot on the back, and smiled like an Olympic Champion.

Taking a second to appraise the couple in front of him, Pilot confidentially told the duo, "Jason, Carly. You two look delightful."

Delightful? Maddie thought.

"Delightful?" Carly questioned, and cocked an eyebrow.

"Come on let's go mingle," Jason stated as he steered Carly

away.

"What was that about?" Maddie questioned Pilot.

"Just waiting for my moment. Plus, she keeps looking back over here. She definitely expected me to mope or fight or something."

"As you should!"

"Yes...but not yet. The party's just beginning."

Maddie laughed as she realized Pilot was acting quite mature. Not to mention Carly really did keep looking over her shoulder. When Pilot decided to ask a seven-year old to dance, Maddie watched Carly's face soften and look as if she would rather be anywhere else than with Jason.

Nancy and Jeremiah strolled into the pavilion to welcoming applause and cheers. Jeesh, those two must get more cheers than an Irish Pub on St. Patty's day, Maddie thought. Maddie was wondering what Howie was up to on his day off, when Nancy---surprisingly---walked over to the table where Maddie was serving drinks and began talking to her.

"Well, hello Madeline."

"Uh, hello Mrs. Gibbz."

"Call me Nancy. Mrs. Gibbz is Cornelious' grandmother's name."

"Right. Er, how are you?" Why do rich people always say things like that? Maddie wondered.

"Wonderful, wonderful. You must know...I don't think your mom is guilty. We have very good lawyers if you need any help."

Taken back by Mrs. Gibbz's generosity and left-field comment Maddie replied, "Oh, yeah. Thanks, we'll consider it."

"Great. Oh! Doesn't Cornelious just look sooo handsome?"

Maddie looked over to the entrance, where a groomed Cornelious stood next to his curly-headed but otherwise similar-looking cousin. "Yes, he does."

As Cornelious stepped into the back pavilion, he was greeted by people he knew, and people he wished he didn't. Of course, Dane was eating this up completely. After a few minutes of maneuvering around the party, Cornelious decided to take a break and chat with Maddie for a while.

With Dane in tow, they headed over to the snowflake bar, where Maddie was serving drinks. Before Cornelious could say anything Dane cut in, "Can I have a 7-7 on the rocks?"

"Sure, when you look old enough to ride a bike," Maddie replied.

"Ouch. Well then, how about seven of my favorite numbers?"

"And what would they be?"

"Your phone number," Dane smiled and Maddie laughed.

Cornelious couldn't believe how cheesy his cousin was acting, and hoped he was kidding. Apparently, he wasn't, for as the minutes passed Dane continued to talk to Maddie about anything and everything. Even after Cornelious announced he was leaving to re-mingle, Dane shrugged him off and replied he wanted to stay where the heat was---

whatever that meant.

Cornelious turned to meet new guests, when he realized there was a slight altercation on the dance floor. He made his way through the slowly-forming crowd and discovered a frantic Carly standing between a smug looking Pilot and an enraged Jason.

"You cannot just waltz up to where MY date and I were standing and kiss MY date on the mouth!" Jason yelled.

"Well, she was standing under mistletoe."

"WITH ME!"

"You didn't make a move," Pilot flashed a winning smile.

"That's because I was planning on making a move later."

"And what does that mean?" Carly stopped holding the two back and crossed her arms.

Realizing he was the center of attention, Jason smirked, "You know. Simple-minded girls usually want one thing from good-looking guys."

"Are you saying I'm EASY?"

"And simple-minded," Pilot added.

Originally, Carly didn't want to make a scene, but now she was too angry to care.

"I didn't say it...you did," Jason laughed at himself.

With no warning and built up years of pent-up anger towards Jason, Pilot stepped past Carly and swiftly punched Jason directly in his face.

Naturally, Jeremiah Gibbz only saw a lunatic ginger-kid (whom he refuses to admit is his son's friend), attack his good friend and esteemed constituent's son. Therefore, he could not fathom why there were cheers, but knew he had to remove the problem from the premises. "SECURITY! GET HIM OUT OF HERE!"

Cornelious knew it would be pointless to argue, and realized Pilot had left the party with Carly. Therefore, he figured everything had ended better than expected for the two of them. Finally, Cornelious thought.

Shortly thereafter, when the party finished, Cornelious headed back over to the snowflake bar where Dane was sitting and staring at Maddie (who was busy cleaning up). "Mads, do you need a ride home?"

"Or you could sleep over..." Dane teased, or at least Cornelious thought he was teasing.

"Neal your cousin's crazy," but Maddie was smiling. "Trent is still somewhere around here...and he said he would drive me home, seeing as Mia left to drive Carly and Pilot home ages ago."

"Right," Cornelious shook his head.

"Did you see Pilot punch Jason?"

"Yup! It was awesome."

"Dang it! I missed it...talking to this kid," Maddie indicated Dane, who smiled sheepishly.

"Let's just say I shouldn't have doubted his ability to protect himself against the Pitbulls," Cornelious proudly proclaimed.

22

"Yet another win-win-win from our mighty Aces. With freshman super standout Cornelious Gibbz leading the way-hey with eighteen points and eleven reboundsssss," sang Ms. Dugan.

Under these circumstances, an average person would allow his newfound popularity to go to his head. But Cornelious had much more on his mind than glory. Besides schoolwork, the group decided they needed to step up their investigation, and agreed to meet at least four times a week. The only upside was that Maddie and he shared all the same classes, so she usually did most of his homework.

"Hey did you guys hear about the concert tonight?" Pilot asked Maddie and Cornelious while they were running laps in gym class.

Cornelious was surprised, "Yeah. My parents are going and keep insisting I tag along to make 'valuable contacts.'"

Maddie laughed, "I don't think that's the concert he's talking about."

Cornelious shrugged, and Pilot added, "I know East Asbury has their prestigious concert for celebrating the New Year, but there's an anti-concert tonight and Jazz is in it."

"Awesome. I'm game."

"Me too. But don't we need tickets?" Maddie inquired.

"Yup. I bought two, for Carly and I---shut up guys, it's our first date---and for some reason, Jazz gave me two extra. I guess he figured you two would come."

"I don't know if Jazz would be too excited to see me," Cornelious said.

"Oh, he only hates East Asburyans who act like East Asburyans."

Cornelious understood what he meant, but he still was uncomfortable with the idea of going to an anti-concert where he may very well be hated for something he had no control over---his wealth. "Yeah, I'll go." Before he could change his mind, Mr. Chase blew his whistle and signaled for the class to break up into teams to play volleyball.

****

Around ten-thirty the most prominent wives of Asbury were putting the finishing touches on their hair or makeup, and asking their husbands to double-check their pockets for the tickets. Within minutes limos would arrive to take the masses to Pecunia Palace for the annual January 7th New Year concert (always exactly a week after New Year's Eve). Inside the Palace, golden drapes covered each window, and clarinets and flutes warmly welcomed each person into the building. Those earning less than an acceptable amount of zeroes need not attend.

On the other side of town, three burly teenagers stood outside the Asbury Junkyard and took pleasure in turning away those without a different type of ticket. In fact, they called themselves The Junkyard Dogs, as affirmed by their demeanor and physical appearance.

"If yous ain't from West As, yous ain't allowed in!" barked one of the dogs.

"Are you sure we'll get in?" Carly asked, nervously biting her nails.

"Yes! Quit worrying," Pilot responded as he stepped up to the dogs and handed them four tickets.

"Hmmm, this seems legit..."

"That's because they are," Carly stated.

"Hey boy, tell your girlfriend here to shut up," scowled another one of the dogs, eyeing up Cornelious.

"She's not with him, she's with me," Pilot retorted. "And you never tell a lady to shut up."

Maddie was about to laugh at Pilot's last comment, but sensed trouble building and intervened. "What he means to say, is just let us in already. Come on Johnny, my dad gave you a sixty-percent discount fixing up that lemon of yours."

The Junkyard Dog named Johnny relented, and directed

the gang to enter the ten-foot high junkpile with the blue flag on top of it, through the giant tire.

Maddie and Cornelious led the way, as Pilot was still fuming about the guard confusing Carly as Cornelious' date. "I guess you should sit next to Cornelious when we get in there."

"I highly doubt we'll be sitting," Maddie said.

"Or maybe you should just dance with him."

Carly turned and faced Pilot, "Ugh, Pi. Stop it. If we wanted to hear you complain, we would have gone to an NBA game or watched that movie you hate so much---"

"Hackers?! Ugh, it's just too unrealistic to think that---"

"Let's just enjoy our date."

Hearing Carly call their date a, well, date made Pilot blush and forget all about the guards, and that ridiculous movie.

The gang made their way through the oversized tire, and were surprised at how bright it was inside. Apparently, the result of constructing a room inside a faux junkpile was not as dreary as the gang had imagined. Lights were strung about on the high ceiling, and seats, couches, and a handful of bean bags were strewn about the room. But the majority of the space was devoted to a large dirt-packed dance floor, with a wooden stage large enough to hold only one band at a time, against the back wall. There was a small concession stand for drinks and water, but it looked vacant tonight.

"Do they have a lot of concerts here?" Cornelious yelled to Maddie, who was right next to him.

"I think...Trent comes here maybe two, three times a

year," Maddie yelled back.

After agreeing to go to the anti-concert, Maddie and Cornelious decided to let Carly and Pilot have their own space and hang with each other.

"Hey, I know those girls," Cornelious said pointing to two girls standing right in front of them.

"Yeah, they're seniors, I think. That one dates Trent's friend Bill, and the other one dates Rodney. Oh God, I sound like Carly."

Before Cornelious could comment, the girls turned around and asked, "Did you guys mention Rodney?"

"Er, yeah. But we---"

"He was supposed to be here fifteen minutes ago. If he blows me off again, I'm going to scream."

Not wanting to hear the girl scream, Maddie and Cornelious slipped away and managed to procure a spot right in front of the stage. And just in time. The opening act was some middle-schoolers who started out nervous, but ended with the crowd yelling encore. There were some good bands, but the best by far was Jazz's band entitled 'The Nooks.' They played an entire set list and two encores.

It was about two in the morning when the anti-concert was over. The gang hung around long enough to congratulate Jazz.

"Man, you did great!"

"Thanks Pilot."

"I think it goes without saying but... I never knew you were that good," Maddie smiled.

Jazz smiled in return and even accepted compliments from Cornelious and Carly.

The group decided to crash at Maddie's, seeing as the Junkyard was down the street from Maddie's development. When the gang reached her house, Pilot's phone began to ring wildly.

"Sshhh, my parents are trying to sleep!"

"Sorry...uh, oh."

The gang looked at Pilot and realized something was wrong.

"Ummm.."

"What?"

"Nothing, it can wait until morning"

Maddie had a sick feeling in her gut, "Tell us now Pilot."

"Well...there's been another break-in...at the Castones. Twenty grand was stolen."

"And..."

"And... well... your mom's name has been released as the prime suspect."

The gang was silent as the news sunk in. "Well, we should go wake up my mom and warn her," Maddie decided.

"Mads, wait. That may not be a good idea. If she knows she's a suspect, they'd ask how she got that info, and it would come back to us and Pilot. And I don't think they're too fond of you guys down there," Cornelious was pulling Maddie back as he spoke.

Knowing it would be best to head upstairs and attempt to get some sleep, they entered the house and began to walk upstairs. Carly halted the group suddenly by saying, "I think I hear police sirens."

Sure enough, within seconds police sirens were wailing outside the Petrozza house.

"Mommmmmyyy!" cried one of the twins.

"What's going on?" Alec yelled from inside his room.

An irritated Mr. Petrozza opened his door and flew down the stairs, crashing into the gang on the way. "What'd you guys do?"

But before they could answer, a hearty knock and loud voice came from outside the door. "Open up! Police."

"Coming! Hold your horses, jeesh," although Mr. Petrozza was trying to sound nonchalant, Carly realized his hands were shaking and his voice seemed higher than usual. "What's this about?"

"Excuse me, we have an arrest warrant for a Mrs. Natalie Petrozza," Officer Chip stated.

"I'm coming, I'm coming," came a strong voice from upstairs. "What's wrong now?"

Officer Chip, although quite the alpha male, saw the twins latched onto their mother, with all the Petrozza kids looking shaken up behind her. Therefore, he decided to make sure the little ones didn't see their mother in handcuffs. After all, he wasn't heartless. "Ma'am, you're going to have to come with us."

"Oh," Mrs. Petrozza realized exactly what was going on now. Unfortunately, so did the media, as news vans began to pull up outside the household.

Mrs. Petrozza kissed each child goodbye, and told them not to worry. She then followed Officer Chip outside and slid into the back of the squad car, with cameras thrust in her face the whole time.

"Who would have thought such a small town could have so many news vans?" Pilot asked trying to lighten the mood.

Maddie turned around to head upstairs when she realized Cornelious was gone. "Did Neal leave?" Maddie asked. Carly and Pilot glanced at each other but only shrugged in reply. Too tired to walk upstairs, the trio crashed in the living room.

****

"This is so embarrassing. Sir," Cornelious said. It was annoying enough Jeremiah Gibbz had called him up and demanded they meet outside Maddie's house. But as soon as he ventured over to meet his dad, the limo driver pushed Cornelious into the backseat, and locked the doors before speeding away.

"The last thing we need is bad publicity. And the Petrozza clan is bad publicity."

"But---"

"No buts! You are not to speak to any of those friends of yours until after this blows over. Or I'll cut you and your 'friends' from the cheer and basketball teams." Cornelious was stunned that his dad could be so heartless as to ruin not just his life, but his two best friends as well. Staring down his father, he knew that Jeremiah Gibbz rarely bluffed, especially when it came to public image.

"What?! You can't do that. Literally." Cornelious knew

how hard Carly and Maddie had worked all year-round, and couldn't imagine them losing their spots on the team all because of him.

"Oh, can't I? One call to Coste, and I think everything will be---"

"Okay, okay. I get it. Sir."

23

Pilot and Carly had been looking forward to their first date for a week, but Cornelious and Maddie agreed it was long overdue. Unfortunately for the two, their first date was memorable, but it wasn't exactly the type of night they liked to recall. It was comparable to remembering the first time you tasted split-pea soup. Although you knew it was something you would never forget, just thinking about it made you queasy. With Mrs. Petrozza's arrest, they decided the weekend should be spent aiding the Petrozza clan in any way they could, and keeping Maddie from freaking out. Especially with the absence of Cornelious---no one knew where he was or how to reach him, and he wasn't picking up his cell.

"I mean, he is my best friend. You'd think he'd be here," Maddie would mutter as she paced in her bedroom.

Carly and Pilot tirelessly tried to steer her mind away from both topics (her mother and Cornelious), but it was no use. After two stressful days of Petrozza children bursting into Maddie's room crying, and Maddie's constant pacing about her room, Pilot and Carly became anxious themselves.

"You know Pi, this week's gonna be rough," Carly whispered, keeping one eye on Maddie.

"I know...but what are we supposed to do? We can only say so much."

****

Pilot and Carly were correct in their predictions of the rough week ahead. Kids, no matter how innocent, could be mean---whether it was making obvious gestures to hide jewelry in Maddie's presence, or poking fun of Trent and Maddie's clothes stating, "Well, we know where the money didn't go."

To make matters worse, Cornelious would barely acknowledge Maddie, let alone offer any words of comfort. In the beginning of the week Maddie tried to pull him aside and give him a piece of her mind. But Jason and Ed, or Alexis would always intervene and allow Cornelious an opportunity to slip away. Frustrated and clueless as to why Cornelious was acting so moronic, she eventually gave up talking to him too.

As the week passed, Maddie almost got into a few fights (if not for Pilot pulling her back), and actually got up and walked out of Mr. McKlien's class. Nobody could really blame her, for McKlien wrote an equation consisting of Natalie Petrozza stealing various numbers from different variables---which were initials of the families who had been robbed. It was probably the cleverest thing Mr. McKlien had ever done---despite the fact that he had spent the entire night thinking it up instead of chatting online with his newest fiancé.

The only silver lining for Maddie was her basketball team. She was extremely lucky to have Willy as such an understanding coach, who allowed no gossip or petty crap to exist in practice. He made sure the team was focused on one thing: winning. Hence, the girls on the team helped Maddie take her mind off of her problems for a while. Unfortunately, Maddie couldn't exactly focus and they ended up losing one of their games, and only won the other by two---thanks to a lucky hook shot from Nya.

Simply put, Maddie couldn't wait for this week to end. On Friday, practice wasn't too long, for the wrestling team had a match and needed the gym. However, Maddie still had a book club meeting to attend, and Cunningham told Maddie the group would wait to meet until after her practice. Having no choice but to attend, Maddie put sweats over her practice jersey, and ran down the hall and into the library. Cunningham was overjoyed to introduce the newest book they were reading---'Six Suspects.' Alexis had snickered that Asbury's police had only needed one. Maddie was too worn-out to retort, so she pretended not to hear, and listened as Milton explained that this was the same author who penned the much-loved Bollywood classic, 'Slumdog Millionaire.' Even though Milton offered her a ride home, Maddie didn't feel like talking, and said she had to grab stuff from her locker because she was meeting up with Pilot at Brady's. Milton looked a little disappointed, but walked Maddie to her locker before turning the corner and walking out the side glass doors near the gymnasium.

Maddie opened her locker and saw someone had left a note that read: GUILTY. Maddie laughed, and thought that maybe kids were losing their creativity and intelligence. Guilty? Seriously?

"Uh, oh guys. Hide your wallets."

"Look, she's laughing at herself. That's the first sign of insanity."

Maddie whirled around to face a group of guys from the basketball team. Cornelious was among them, but made a point of staring a hole through the floor. Maddie tried to catch his eye, but knew it would be pointless. Maybe this weekend she would show up at his house, and demand an explanation.

"What? You can't even think of a comeback? Just three days ago you were ready to pounce on me! I don't know how that ginger friend of yours managed to hold you back."

Maddie remembered exactly what the blonde-haired junior was talking about. Although she didn't know his name, Maddie wanted to rip his throat out the other day when he mentioned his lawyer-dad placing Sophia, Shannon, and Daniel into a safer home.

"Well, I'll remind my ginger friend..." Maddie said making a point of looking at Cornelious, "not to make that mistake again."

"Is that a threat? Maybe they should throw you in jail with your mom."

"No way, Ed. They should stick her in a loony-bin. Ya know, white padded rooms."

"You know, you're right. Just give me your address and I'll move in," Maddie grabbed her books and closed her locker.

It took the guys a few minutes to realize she had insulted them.

"Don't listen to her dude. She's not worth it. I know, it's a waste for such a cute face," Ed laughed at his own joke, which no one else thought was funny. "C'mon guys, I just rhymed."

"So you did pass the first grade. I always wondered..." Maddie stated. "Oh, and Ed, it's funny YOU should be the one to say I was insane for 'laughing at myself', seeing as you're always laughing at your own dumb jokes, because no one else thinks you're funny."

Ed turned as red as Rudolph's nose, and stepped back as two other guys on the team stepped closer to Maddie. "I see what you mean now Ed. She thinks she's a jokester."

"Yeah, I hope you tell your mommy jokes in jail. It'll probably make her feel better, huh?"

Maddie decided she had had enough and attempted to walk away, but realized the team had blocked the hallway to the glass doors.

"Yeah. And if your dad needs some help paying bills, my offer still stands to hire you as a maid or---"

"SHUT UP!"

Maddie and Cornelious were stunned to see that Eric
Henry had walked up to the group and was now yelling at his
own team. It's common knowledge that Eric was eager to
impress his teammates, seeing as he was only a freshman who
occasionally played up on Varsity. Therefore, pretty much
everyone thought they had misunderstood his interruption.
The group even stepped aside and looked at Eric, hoping he
would explain himself or adjust his prior outburst.

Coming from down the hall, Eric heard them taunt
Maddie for a few minutes, and couldn't believe why
Cornelious was just standing there. "Seriously, you guys need
to get a life. It's innocent 'til proven guilty. You guys should
know by now that our police suck, and make more mistakes
than...than...Michael Jackson's plastic surgeon. Why would
the Petrozzas steal anything? And if they did where's the
money? Evidence? Motive?"

Cornelious couldn't believe that Eric had the guts to stand
up to the upperclassmen. Apparently, neither could the
upperclassmen. After a speechless response, Eric grabbed
Maddie's hand and they walked through the group and out
the doors. The team immediately discussed Eric's sudden
change of character.

"Weird."

"I actually think I respect Henry for standing up to us."

"True, maybe we should invite him to the next party."

"No way! He'd bring his new convict girlfriend."

The group began discussing the next party at some girl

name Tiffany's, but Cornelious wasn't feeling too chatty. He told the gang he would see them Monday, and decided to head to Brady's. As he walked down the boardwalk, he realized he wasn't mad at Eric for standing up to those jerks, but he was mad at himself for not stepping in first.

Cornelious walked into Brady's to see a busy Ms. Owens scurrying around the restaurant. "Oh, Neal! I didn't realize you were coming. Maddie and that Henry boy are right back there in the corner booth. I'm sorry, got to go. Some of your teachers are here today. How cute!"

Cornelious glanced over and saw his econ teacher, guidance counselor, history teacher, and a bunch of teachers he didn't know or didn't have, yet. Not wanting to make small talk, Cornelious meandered over to the back corner. "Uh, hey guys."

Up until now, Maddie had hated Eric Henry. But after what had happened, she decided she had misjudged him, and that maybe he did deserve a second chance. Maddie asked Eric why he had stood up for her, but he had only shrugged and replied that he owed her. Just as the two were settling down to eat, they were interrupted by someone she would rather ignore.

Eric felt the tension between the two buds, and looked at his watch. "Jeez, I was supposed to be home at seven!" Eric quickly got up and left Brady's.

"It's only five forty-five!" Maddie called after him. "What do you want?" Maddie turned her attention back to Cornelious as he slid into the booth.

"Listen, please. I'm sorry. I've been a jerk. It's just my dad threatened to---"

"Puh--leezz. Since when have you listened to your dad? You just want to make sure you were in good standing with your basketball buddies," Maddie retorted, getting up from the booth.

"Mads, Maddie..." Cornelious reached for her sleeve and pulled her back down. "Madeline Isabella---"

"Okay, okay. Don't start saying my full name," Maddie looked around to make sure no one had heard. "Especially not now, since the Pitbulls arrived."

Cornelious looked over his shoulder and saw the unruly gang take their place in the booth behind them. "Mads, I'm so extremely sorry. I will never... I'll always have your back. You know me, right? I'm sorry."

Maddie saw how sorry Cornelious appeared. She considered him for a moment and then sat up straight, motioning Ms. Owens over.

"Well, I guess it's just you two now, eh?"

"Yeah, Carly had cheerleading and Pilot is, er..."

"Yes, I know. He's volunteering for the elderly. He's so sweet," Ms. Owens gushed.

Cornelious and Maddie looked at each other and tried their hardest not to laugh. They quickly ordered peanut butter and chocolate pancakes---Cornelious' treat---and burst out laughing when Ms. Owens had left the vicinity.

"Pilot? And old folk?"

"That's just too much!"

Unbeknownst to the duo, Pilot was, in a sense, volunteering his time for the elderly. In his fortified room, running an undetectable program, Pilot thought it would be fun to pass the time by giving anyone over sixty-five in the United States free healthcare. Leaning back, he couldn't wait to catch the nightly news later and watch D.C. implode like Mrs. Cosentino's famous honey custard cake.

By the time Ms. Owens had dropped off their dinner (or breakfast), Maddie and Cornelious had made up and were discussing this past week.

"Wait, wait. Ssshhh," Maddie suddenly whispered.

"What?"

"I just heard the Pitbulls mention jewelry."

"You heard that?" Cornelious asked amazed.

"Yes! Ssshhh!"

Cornelious knew he was lucky Maddie had forgiven him so easily, and didn't want to spoil anything. Not wanting to waste any time, Maddie quickly got up and slid next to Cornelious, as to better hear the Pitbulls' conversation behind them.

"I know! I can NOT believe what they paid for these suckers!"

"They're the real suckers."

"JB you ARE the MAN!"

"I know, I know... No one else could've gotten anyone to fork over a grand, let alone eight-grand, for costume jewelry."

The Pitbulls began to laugh and pound on their tables so loudly, that Brandan and Dennis had to come out from the kitchen and ask them to leave 'me restaurant'---desperately trying to retain some of their Irish ethnicity.

When Maddie and Cornelious were sure the Pitbulls had left Brady's, they faced each other, and Cornelious voiced what they both were thinking. "So that jewelry you saw was, what did they say? Costume jewelry?"

"Ahh. It's makes sense," Maddie stated dejectedly. "Costume jewelry looks real, but it's just synthesized stones, and base metals, and glass, and plastic."

Cornelious knew better by now than to ask her how she knew this information. "So this means, er...they're innocent?"

Maddie knew Cornelious was trying to ask politely, and also knew that he wasn't the type of person to say 'I told you so.' Still, she felt idiotic.

"Ugh, you were right! They have nothing to do with this. They were just my... my red herring." After a moment of silence, Maddie added, "So now I guess we have no suspects."

"Not yet. But we will," Cornelious promised his best friend.

24

With Mrs. Petrozza released from police custody for about three weeks now, Maddie had to eat every meal with her family, and be at home by six. Therefore, she jumped at the opportunity to help Carly and Pilot with their first Valentine's Day date.

"I love holidays." Carly swooned as she tried on different outfits from her mini-mall-like-closet, and tossed them aside in disgust.

"Me too. But today doesn't really count." Maddie added as she lay upside-down on Carly's bed, taking no interest in her friend's excitement.

Carly turned around and glared at Maddie. "Well for one, with your head hanging off my bed, the blood's probably ran

into your head and you're too confused. And for another---"
Maddie cut her off to laugh, "you don't realize it's importance
because you don't have a date."

"Exactly! Valentine's Day isn't universally fun for
everyone, so it shouldn't be considered a holiday. Just an
excuse to demand chocolate and compliments from loved
ones. Or ones you think love you, or you think you love."

Carly ignored Maddie and decided on a pinkish (Carly said
coral), dress that twirled when she moved a certain way. And
she made sure to move that way as much as possible. "I just
don't know whether to curl my hair, or straighten it."

"It's already straight," Maddie pointed out.

"Ugh, you know nothing.... I'll curl it."

What seemed like centuries later, Maddie looked at her
watch and was glad to see it was seven. The plan was for
Cornelious and Pilot to arrive in Cornelious' limo, at precisely
seven-fifteen. The girls would be waiting outside, so Mr. and
Mrs. Cosentino wouldn't have time to snap too many shots.
Cornelious would then give the driver over to the Pilot---to
follow his every whim---and Maddie and Cornelious would
take the trolley to the arcade or Brady's to kill time.

At seven-fifteen, Maddie grabbed Carly and pulled her
outside, with Mr. and Mrs. Cosentino following close behind.
No joke, close to two hundred shots were taken in less than
three minutes. Cornelious joked that Carly's parents had to be
paparazzis in a past life.

"See ya guys!"

"Have fun sweetie!"

With all the planning and helping their friends, Maddie and Cornelious realized how hungry they had become. They waved goodbye to the Cosentinos and made their way out of the Caldwell Courts community. Luckily, they only had to walk half a block before the trolley picked them up outside the Saratelli's mansion.

Once inside Brady's, they almost turned around and left. But Maddie was too hungry to care that almost every customer was on a date, and the only seat left was the booth by the kitchen's swinging door.

"I'm way too hungry. I'll even get the seat closest to the kitchen door."

Cornelious laughed and agreed, "As long as you're the one getting hit by the waitresses and not me."

Ms. Owens may have been busy tonight, but her smile shone brighter than the North Star. "Hello, you two! I cannot believe my little Pi-Pi is on a date! Who knew six months into high school would mature him so fast?"

They laughed and Ms. Owens left to bring them some taco pancakes. Maddie and Cornelious shared stories of Pi-Pi and Carly's pre-date behavior.

"Carly must've tried on at least five hundred outfits! And at one point she only curled half her hair, before deciding maybe she should cut it short---don't worry I saved her from that one."

"You think that's crazy? Pilot wanted to dye his hair brown and bring a mini-computer with him to make sure he didn't say the wrong things...Let's say I only succeeded in preventing one of the two."

"He did NOT bring a computer with him?! Did he?"
Maddie stared in horror.

"Yup. But we know Carly. She'll probably make him throw
it out. Shame too, it looked expensive."

"I bet he built it himself."

Ms. Owens came back looking a little flustered and
dropped off two steaming hot, taco pancakes with syrup on
the side. "Uh, here's your order."

"What's wrong Ms. O?"

"Well, Neal, Little Miss Miserable to the left won't stop
crying about how her boyfriend stood her up and that she
loved him and now they're over. She's scaring away
customers. But I feel too awful to kick her out."

"Rough."

"Yeah, I know. But this kid must be a jerk to break
someone's heart on Valentine's Day."

Cornelious looked over and thought he recognized the girl
from somewhere other than school. She probably just dated
one of his teammates or something, Cornelious thought and
shrugged it off. Not caring to look, Maddie stuffed her face as
Ms. Owens grabbed a box of kleenex from the counter, and
headed over to (hopefully) end the waterworks.

Cornelious looked over his meal and said his usual, "It's a
taco hidden in a pancake, who knew?"

Before Cornelious could fully appreciate his first bite,
Maddie spit out her food.

"Ew. What? Is it uncooked or something." Cornelious

lifted up his meal, to inspect his taco pancake.

"What?! No, it's delicious. Better than usual actually. Mostly because I think this time they added a little---

"Mads. You're killing me. Why did you spit out perfectly good food all over me then?"

"Sorry!" Maddie apologized quickly. Then she glanced both ways, to make sure no one was listening, and motioned for Cornelious to lean in closer. "You just solved a crucial part of the case, and I'm sure of it! No one else, not even the police, suspect what you have just unearthed."

Cornelious was shocked, but he had no idea what Maddie meant.

"Don't you see? This taco pancake is exactly like the surprise reporter from your Thanksgiving dinner."

"Huh? I don't follow. Unless you mean they're both meaty. But that doesn't make sense---"

"No!" Maddie whispered even lower, "The taco is hidden in the pancake (as you pointed out), and the reporter was hidden in your wicker closet."

Cornelious was beginning to understand her thought process. "So, the thief must've been hiding in the house, prior to the thefts!"

"Yes! He probably hid somewhere the night or day before, and chose the best possible moment to steal."

"So he could start robbing and then hide, if he heard someone."

"We have to tell Carly and Pilot."

"Let's just text them to meet at your place after their date."

The duo agreed and downed their taco pancakes as quickly as humanly possible. Once they made sure to pay and tip handsomely (for it was Ms. Owens), they hurried down the boardwalk, hopped the trolley, and sprinted into the Petrozza household. Once inside, Cornelious skid to a halt causing Maddie to run right into him and fall backwards.

"Ouch! What's the big idea?"

Cornelious replied with the one word that confused Maddie so much, she couldn't speak, "Mom?"

In all their years of friendship, neither Gibbz parent had ever dared to venture into any West Asbury house, let alone her own. Cornelious bent down to help Maddie up, and walked into the living room where his mother and the Petrozza parents were sitting, along with a cheesy-looking man with a long nose and one eyebrow, holding a briefcase.

"Oh. Hello dear. You remember Mr. Carow?"

"Yes. How could I forget our beloved family attorney? But why is he here?"

"Well, your father may be in a pissy mood, but ever since you stood up to him a month ago and told him to call Coste and kick you, Carly and Maddie off from their teams, I realized I should follow your example." Nancy Gibbz turned back to the Petrozzas. "You have to know Natalie, that I always believed you were---are innocent. Therefore, if need be, I am offering---insisting that you use our attorney to assist you. Don't worry, this deal is all-expenses-paid."

Nancy Gibbz walked over to Natalie and bear-hugged her. Maddie and Cornelious decided this was an adult matter---

and uncomfortable one too, seeing as Nancy was still wrapped around Natalie as the two made their way into Maddie's room.

"Wow."

"Thank you," Maddie replied as she did her own impression of Nancy's bear hug.

"Yeah yeah. Now get off me," Cornelious laughed, turning red with sudden embarrassment.

"Seriously though… why didn't you tell me that your dad threatened all of us?" Maddie looked at Cornelious, and finally got a glimpse of just how much pressure his father put on him.

Cornelious shrugged, "I wasn't about to add that to your plate too… besides, after Eric stood up to the Varsity, I went home and told him to call Coste and cut us all. I'm not his puppet and wasn't about to lose you." Feeling his face redden, he quickly added, "And Carly too… of course."

Smiling at her best friend, she hugged him once more, before stepping back and chuckling, "You know, your attorney looks almost bird-like, it's pretty unnerving. I don't think I saw him blink."

"Exactly. That's why my dad hired him, and that's why I call him The Crow. Plus, his last name basically sounds like crow anyway."

Opening the door into Maddie's room, the two got their second surprise of the night. Carly and Pilot were sitting on Maddie's bed, holding hands and looking anxious.

"Don't tell me you guys eloped?" Maddie joked.

Carly looked up at the two and smiled, "Of course not! But we have good news."

Not waiting for Cornelious or Maddie to come up with another joke, Pilot butt right in. "There's been another theft at the Lasbernes!"

"And that's good news because..."

"Because Neal, Mrs. Petrozza---aka your mom Maddie--- was clearly seen by many on a date with her husband, enjoying a meal---"

"At the same restaurant as us," Pilot boasted.

Carly continued smiling at Pilot, "enjoying a meal, during the exact same time of the robbery!"

25

With as bad of a week Maddie (and undoubtedly each Petrozza child) had experienced last month, it was nice to experience a week full of apologies and fellow peers stating how they 'knew she was innocent all along,' many, many times. Every time Maddie opened her locker, she wondered whether she was going to find notebook paper with the words, INNOCENT scribbled on it. But, she guessed, maybe that person still thought wrong.

Some teachers had pulled her aside and offered words of encouragement (clearly trying to make up for their condescending attitudes earlier). Ms. Moskow simply hugged Maddie, and stated, "I knew she was innocent. Let us remember, those who are wrongly persecuted oftentimes end up legends or heroes."

"It wasn't that big of a deal," Alexis muttered, jealous of all the attention and sympathy Maddie now garnered from the teaching staff.

Ms. Moskow looked her classroom over (and in particular Alexis) and sagely said, "It may not be a big deal for those with small minds. For those with small minds often forget, what those with open minds allow themselves to retain."

Cornelious smiled as he realized Ms. Moskow was a pretty cool teacher. As weird as the day is long, but pretty darn cool. When school ended that week, Cornelious drew the conclusion that a lot of people in Asbury must have pretty small minds. Almost everyone claimed they knew Mrs. Petrozza was innocent all along (including his father, who had boasted they had hired her the best attorney to make sure no injustices occurred). Even though Cornelious never thought she was guilty, he hadn't forgiven himself for not being there for his bud. Especially since Eric had now become a staple in their study hall, and made an effort to sit next to Maddie. Cornelious liked Eric and knew Maddie had forgiven him for last year's incident, but he still found his presence slightly annoying at times. Perhaps, he didn't like to mix his best friends with FA (father-approving) ones.

"Annndd just remember-ember, to have a safe and happy, and happy and safe weekend weekend," sang the PA system.

The gang gathered their bags and actually left the school together.

Pilot smiled, "I can't believe you guys all have off from practice today. This has got to be the first free Friday in months!"

"I know! No yelling or flipping or fighting or hitting..." Carly pointed out.

"Is that really what your practices are like?" Cornelious asked.

"Of course. There's always at least two fights. People just can't get their minds around the fact that when someone flips off the pile, someone has to be there to catch them," Carly shook her head.

"Sign me up to watch the next practice."

"Me too!"

"Boys," agreed Carly and Maddie, who just looked at each other.

"What? It's not our fault. It's written in our DNA."

"Yup, right between the double-helix is the phrase 'girl-fight'," Pilot stated.

"Hey, next time we fight we should call them up," Carly teased.

"Good idea," Maddie agreed.

"Seriously?" Pilot asked.

The gang laughed and headed into Split Park on the side of the high school. Some elderly citizens were strolling through the park, and some younger ones were horsing around.

"Hmm, I guess Betty Michaels does dye her hair blue every Friday."

"Huh?" Pilot asked completely bewildered. Maddie laughed but didn't have a chance to explain.

"Look! There's Trent!" Cornelious said, running into the road and asking Maddie's brother if they could hitch a ride.

"Sorry there isn't any room," laughed Trent.

Maddie peered in and saw his two friends, Dave and Kyle, waving from inside the car. "Are you kidding me? There's two open seats."

"Just let them in man, we're missing the race. Plus, Rodney just jumped out anyway---like usual," the dark-headed meathead, Dave added.

"Aww you know him, he's probably at some girl's house. He's been.... preoccupied this year," smiled Trent. After some debate, and seeing as there were already two others in the car, Trent consented to letting in two. "Besides, Mia is behind me and she's coming over. So, two of you go with her." Trent smiled knowing full well it would be safer to ride under Mia's car than inside of it.

After a moment's discussion, it was decided that the boys would go with Trent and the girls would take their chances with Mia. Especially after Carly pleaded with Maddie saying, "C'mon, it's not that bad."

For the average driver, it took about twenty minutes (with lights and stop signs), to get from the park to Maddie's. For Crazy Eddie it took about five. For Mia Cosentino it took nine minutes, and almost two trips to the ER. Therefore, Maddie leapt from the car as soon as she saw her front yard, and waited for the boys to pull up. Ten minutes later the boys ripped open the front door, and Trent scooped up Mia and started laughing.

"Each time I heard an ambulance, I prayed for you guys."

Mia pouted, "Hmph! I'm a good driver!"

The gang decided to sneak away from Trent and Mia and head upstairs. Throwing their book bags into the corner of Maddie's room, the gang broke open the Gushers, Doritos, and Yoohoo---previously stored in Maddie's room for times like this.

"Okay, okay time to get down to business," Maddie stood up and brushed the crumbs off her shirt.

"Agreed. So, what's our plans for tonight? I think Alexis is having a small get-together."

Maddie, Cornelious, and Pilot looked at her blankly. "Alright, I'm just stating the options. Don't shoot me or anything."

"Seeing as that's a terrible idea, I think we should continue working on the case."

"We are still in high school. Let's enjoy ourselves," Carly complained. "Plus, we are getting absolutely nowhere with this investigation."

"C'mon Car. We have an advantage. Remember? The theory that the thief was hiding inside already and waited until everyone left to begin," Pilot stated.

"Well, that may explain why there were no signs of a break-in, but we don't have suspects, motives, or evidence," Carly listed.

"True. Which is why we need to buckle down." Maddie walked over to the giant notepad on the easel and ripped out the old page filled with crossed-out theories and ideas. "First, we need to discover the pattern."

The gang nodded in agreement.

"And today we should test our theory."

"How?" Carly questioned.

"We need to go the houses that were robbed and ask if they let someone into their house earlier that day, but never actually saw him leave. If they say yes, then we know we must be right!"

"But who's gonna answer questions from a bunch of 14 and 15 year-olds?" Carly continued.

"Well, I'll be fifteen in a month," Maddie added.

"Regardless, who would actually listen to us? Huh?"

The group considered this problem, but Cornelious realized the answer was clear. "Of course, the rich wouldn't take the time of day to answer our questions...but the Help would. They love to gossip."

Carly began to grow excited, "Oh my gosh! You're right! Although my parents don't pay anyone to do anything---their idea of teaching us a lesson---our family in Dublin has Help for every little task! And they love to talk to anyone who'll listen. You should see them talk to my deaf and blind Uncle Barry. Poor thing, he doesn't even realize. Nor do they, really."

The next course of action was to break up into pairs with an East-sider in each pair, for credibility. Carly and Pilot agreed to question the Help at the Tibbitts' and Castone's (seeing as they were about two blocks away from each other. Thus, Maddie and Cornelious were set to question the

Lomling's, Lasbernes', and Wallabee's Help. Before setting out on bikes, Carly reminded them to "Ask if the person had a cat."

After a minute's confusion, and wondering if they had heard Carly wrong, she clarified, "Because of the cat hair evident at the crime scenes."

By the time Maddie and Cornelious had reached the first house, they had grown anxious.

"What if the Lomlings answer the door and recognize us, or call the cops?"

"Chillax, Neal. We'll be fine."

The two parked their bikes on the curb and walked up the stone pathway to the Lomling's door. A petite red-haired woman answered the door. "Uh, are you like here for the pool?"

In February? Maddie thought. "Er, no. Sorry. But we were wondering---"

"Sorry, hon. I ain't buying nothing."

"Well, since that's a double negative---" Maddie began, shaking her head.

"Hmm, excuse us. But we're here to exchange some gossip from my maid, Charlene." Cornelious interrupted saving the day.

"Oh! Char! Of course!" the petite red-head now gave them her full attention.

"Cool. You see, Char was wondering if you had, er, let a boy into the house a while ago. One you never really saw leave?"

"Like a ghost?" the maid asked confused.

"No, er---" Cornelious looked imploringly at Maddie.

"What he means to ask, is did you let a boy into the house a while back? And a cat too?" she added on a side note.

"A cat? Hmm...I don't...Oh wait! Yes, I did. Good looking boy too! Poor thing, he was crying over his lost cat. Said it meant the world to him, and that his mom gave it to him before she passed. You don't forget something like that. He said it climbed in through the window and wanted to know if he could look around inside real quick. What could I do? I love cats!"

Cornelious and Maddie were amazed. Not only had this lady admitted to letting their new suspect in, but Carly had been right in her insistence on the importance of cat hairs. They knew they would never hear the end of this.

"Tell Char not to mention the cat to anyone. My boss is pretty scared of them, ya know?"

"Yeah, well thanks for your help. You said it was a good-looking boy, a teenager?"

"Yup...why?"

"It may have been Charlene's nephew. They, er, lost the cat. Again," Cornelious sadly shook her head.

"Poor baby!"

Two hours later, the gang met up again in Maddie's room. Not only had each housemaid provided the same sob story about a boy's lost cat, but they had a basic sketch for a suspect.

"Should we tell the police?" Carly asked.

"No way! They'd botch this up and scare the thief!"

"True, Pi. Plus, they also wouldn't listen to us, even if we caught the thief red-handed," Maddie realized.

"Which is what we're gonna have to do," Cornelious pointed out.

"So all we need is a pattern, and we'll have him caught in no time," Pilot decided.

"Assuming he's not finished robbing houses in Asbury already," Carly ominously stated.

26

Weeks passed and the gang surly realized they were stuck.
Yes, they agreed their theory of a teenage boy sneaking into
the houses on the premise of locating a lost cat, was most
likely correct and pretty logical. But no matter how many
ideas were thrown about, no one knew how to catch the thief
in the act. Carly had suggested a couple of times that maybe
the thief had decided enough was enough, and simply moved
on. But Pilot insisted he had a gut feeling the robberies were
not over yet. To Carly's dismay, Maddie and Cornelious sided
with Pilot and the gang continued to work to figure out the
thief's pattern.

On March Eighth, the day after Maddie's fifteenth
birthday, the group found themselves sitting quietly in study
hall. Maddie was typing a composition for Economics, while
correcting Carly's English thesis. Carly was busy mentally
practicing a new cheer, while Cornelious was attempting to

do some Geometry proofs, muttering "I really hate these things. Pointless."

Pilot, on the other hand, was the only one currently going through the case in his mind. He knew there was something obvious he had missed. If only he could figure it out! While he was trying to piece together a possible pattern or suspect, he realized he had been drawing on the past year's 'Fortune Fine 25'. He was about to complain about what a piece of trash this paper was, when a thought abruptly sprang into his mind. Quickly, Pilot scanned the list, pulled out a notebook, and began furiously jotting down notes.

"Hey, uh, Maddie..."

The gang looked up (except for Pilot who was too entrenched in his work), and saw a bored looking Jason standing next to an apologetic-looking Eric.

"What's up?" Maddie asked.

"Ms. Clarke, er, wanted you to come in yesterday to guidance." Eric looked uncomfortable, as if he was afraid to make her upset.

"Oh, well, it was my birthday first of all. And second of all, I'm not going to anymore guidance counselor meetings or talks or whatever. And she asks too many darn questions."

"Darn? Still afraid to curse?" Jason laughed and began flexing as he saw a group of sophomores pass.

Eric rolled his eyes at Jason, and continued, "That's pretty much what I thought, so I told her and she said you need signed parental consent."

"To stop going? Okay, I'll bring it in tomorrow...what's the big deal?"

"She probably thinks no one takes her seriously," Carly answered.

"Yeah, well she never asked me to go," Pilot muttered as he stopped writing and looked up.

"That's because you're not important enough to talk to," Jason smiled.

Before anyone could reply Carly arched her eyebrows to glare at Jason, turned to Pilot and kissed him smack on the lips. Predictably, Jason grunted, pulled Eric to his side, and quickly left the library. Pilot smiled victoriously, and the gang got back to their work.

Almost forgetting what he was previously doing, Pilot glanced at his notebook and picked up right where he left off. After about five minutes, Pilot had finished writing in his notebook and looked eagerly at each member of the group.

Cornelious had looked up when Pilot was about halfway through his note-taking, and wondered what his friend was doing. It was only after Pilot had finished scribbling notes, that Cornelious recognized the crazed look in his friend's wild green eyes.

"Guys, I think Pilot's gone crazy."

"No, he's always been that way." Carly stated nonchalantly and continued silently clapping her hands, and mouthing the words to a new cheer.

Pilot began to laugh, which startled Maddie and Carly out of their work-induced trance.

"What the---?" Maddie questioned.

"Pilot Owens! Stop your laughing this instant, or you will be removed from my library!" Mrs. Cunningham threatened.

Pilot managed to control himself and then smiled at the group.

"Don't make us beg, Pilot Owens," Carly warned.

"Oh, I won't...I just discovered," Pilot anxiously looked around the library to ensure nobody was eavesdropping (not that upperclassmen cared enough to listen to freshmen gossip), 'the thief's pattern.'

"No flippin' way!" Maddie exclaimed.

Pilot made sure to drop his voice even lower, and showed the group the magazine he was looking at. "Do you recognize this?"

"Yes. It's the Asbury Fortune Fine 25. The top 25 richest families in Asbury," Carly stated as if rehearsed.

"You are, as usual, one hundred percent correct," Pilot said, and Carly blushed. "But what we've all failed to see is...that this is also the thief's hit list."

Maddie grabbed the magazine and shrugged, "I don't see any pattern. I mean it's not like he's skipping every other name. Then Schoyer or Mentzer would be the starting point."

Pilot nodded, and carried on, "At first, I thought so too. But then I read that of the twenty-five families, thirteen boast of keeping their 'most valuable assets' at home due to distrust in the banks. Thus, we can safely remove twelve names." Taking a permanent marker, Pilot crossed out twelve family names.

"But then we still have thirteen families," Maddie pointed

out.

"Yes, but if you read the actual article, it exhibits snapshots of the 'valuable assets.'" Pilot flipped through the magazine, revealing various photos. "And, Fortune Fine also provides insider details about the interior designs of the houses, or mansions, belonging to seven of the thirteen families... rich people are stupid."

"Or cocky," Maddie added as a side note, seeing as they were friends with two of the top five richest families in town.

Despite Pilot's last statement, the gang was beginning to feel the excitement. So Pilot continued, "And of these seven, five have been robbed thus far!"

Pilot's hypothesis was way too logical for anyone to ignore. The gang triple-checked his pattern-theory, and realized he was spot on.

"Wait, this means Eric's going to be robbed next!" Carly proclaimed.

"Yup, and then..." Pilot began.

"I'm last," Cornelious stated.

****

Although the gang was fairly certain they had discovered the pattern, they still were clueless as to when the thief would strike next. With both teams losing in the state playoffs (the girls had only won the first two games, but the boys had made it to the semis, losing to Shabazz), the foursome now had plenty of free time on their hands. Seeing as nobody played a spring sport---cheerleading included---they tried to focus all of their attention on the case.

Making their way through the crowded cafeteria to their usual seats proved rather difficult today. Student Council had apparently thought it was smart to hang up Spring Fling posters during lunch period. Peetie was looking completely stressed and was yelling at kids to keep moving and clear the aisles. Honestly, school dances don't usually cause this much excitement for students, because most people usually go with a group of friends. But the fact that all of the signs read: 'GIRLS QUIT GAWKIN', IT'S SADIE HAWKINS!', increased female fervor as many began to plot which student to ask, and how to build up the nerve to do so.

Seemingly, the only students unaffected by the madness inspired by the first Sadie Hawkins dance in school history, were Carly, Pilot, Cornelious, and Maddie. Instead, they were fruitlessly trying to list possible suspects--- which was the only area they had failed to make any headway.

"Maybe we can check up on who gets a Fortune Fine subscription," Cornelious proposed.

"I can look that up now," Pilot stated, pulling out his cell.

"Nah, it's free and we didn't even have to get a copy to see it. We grabbed the library's copy, remember?" Maddie said.

"Yeah. Ugh, this is so frustrating. We know the how and the where. We just need the who and the when."

Immediately after Cornelious had spoken, Pilot's cell went haywire. Because Pilot's cell-alarm was fairly loud and a little obnoxious, the gang began to draw looks from fellow peers.

From the table behind them, an annoying curly red-head turned around and poked her head in their conversation.

"Seriously, Owens. Do you have to be such a geek?"

"Alexis!" Carly exclaimed.

"C'mon, Car. It's true. I don't care that you're dating now. Just tell him to turn off that alarm." And on second thought she added, "And get a hair-cut."

"I like his hair. It reminds me of summer," Hannah added, turning around.

As usual, Hannah's out-there comment made the gang laugh.

"Hmph!" Alexis turned to continue her conversation on the proper way to chew gum.

Noticing that there was only about four minutes left in lunch, Pilot quickly broke the news that the Henry's had been robbed the previous night. Hence, the reason for his cell's blaring alarm.

"So that's why he wasn't in school today," Maddie said.

"Poor kid," Carly agreed as she picked at her egg salad.

Pilot squinted at his girlfriend, "I thought you hated him."

"Well, that's because Maddie didn't like him. But since they're friends now, well, everything's changed. Ya know, girl code." Maddie and Carly laughed and pounded it, as the boys looked on bewildered.

"And you say boys are strange," Cornelious muttered.

When the bell rang signaling the end of lunch, Maddie and Cornelious met up with the Peters twins and walked with them to history. Jazz was playing with his guitar string the entire time, and Peetie was busy discussing various things on her agenda that she wished to change about the school.

Although Maddie and Cornelious couldn't honestly care less, they nodded their heads in agreement, and occasionally said "Yeah, totally."

Mr. Caulfield was in an excited mood when the students entered his classroom.

"Maybe he brought in some candies," Cornelious whispered.

"Hopefully."

When each student had taken their seats, Mr. Caulfield began. "We have some very interesting news today. I have just received a phone call from the Food Network and they want to film a segment on my candies this coming summer!"

The class began to murmur in excitement.

Mr. Caulfield continued, "I know that summer is three months away, but it will be here before you know it. The Food Network wants me to come up with my own slogan and art design. I told them that, seeing as I am an educator first and foremost, I will leave it up to my kids. Therefore, the next assignment is to use a historical reference in creating a slogan and design for my candies. Not only will the winners receive one hundred dollars each, but their work will be featured---along with themselves---on national television!"

Now, one hundred dollars may not go too far today, but the chance for fame is always cause for excitement. Without a minute to lose, students began picking partners. Cornelious knew that neither he nor Maddie was particularly artistic, but maybe they would kill it with a slogan. Back in the day they used to come up with little raps, and battle each other.

Cornelious turned to share an idea with Maddie, when he realized her hand was up.

"Yes, Maddie?" asked Mr. Caulfield.

"Er, can I be partners with Eric Henry? He's absent today, but I could head to his house and explain the rules, and stuff."

"How thoughtful. I thought you two were partners. But neither of you are, uh, skilled in the arts, eh?" Mr. Caulfield said, indicating Cornelious and Maddie.

"Yeah. We're not the best," Maddie smirked.

Mr. Caulfield smiled and clapped his hands together. "Okay. Students! I want this project handed into me no later than April Thirtieth. I believe that is plenty of time."

Knowing it would be useless to try to wrangle the class together for a lesson after the announcement, Mr. Caulfield sat at his desk and graded tests, as students talked excitedly and chose partners. Cornelious was a little tiffed that Maddie had chosen Eric as a partner over himself, and walked around the room looking for a worthy partner, so he could beat Maddie and Eric.

After the list was circulated and partners signed up, many of the girls were shocked and reasonably jealous to see Cornelious' partner. Of course, they would never had asked him themselves, but they had each secretly hoped he would have approached them. If Cornelious had realized what they were thinking, he would have definitely chosen any one of them over his current partner, Brittney Anne Saratelli. Brittney Anne Saratelli appeared very condescending to those who didn't know her---mainly due to the extremely small glasses she insisted on keeping perched right above the edge of her nose. Unfortunately for Cornelious, not only was she indeed condescending, but also she was very annoying. Upon agreeing to their partnership, Brittney Anne wrote down the specific dates and times of availability, and insisted that he make as many as possible, stating "I know you probably have hazel eyes over there do everything for you..." she nodded to Maddie.

Hazel eyes? Cornelious thought, smirking.

"And seeing as you'll probably make up excuses not to come, let's just save time. I'll do the project, and you can give me, oh, fifty bucks."

After a few minutes of tirelessly explaining to Brittney Anne that he wouldn't be paying fifty bucks and intends to fully work on the project, Brittney Anne rolled her eyes (causing her glasses to nearly fall off), and agreed to four days in April to work on the project.

When the class piled out of the door, Cornelious grabbed Maddie by the shoulder and thanked her for leaving him stuck with Saratelli.

"Oh, I'm sorry. I bet if you asked anyone else, they would've said yes."

"Yeah, well, I didn't. And why the sudden interest in Eric? This time last year you were ready to kill him."

"I can't believe I have to explain myself... I thought it was obvious." Maddie looked around, and pushed Cornelious against the lockers, so they could talk in private.

Cornelious exhaled and crossed his arms across his chest, "I'm listening."

Maddie looked around, leaned in and whispered, "By being his partner, I can show up to his house, and ask him to show me around a little. I'd look for clues---discreetly, of course---and maybe find something we missed. If you went and asked for a tour he'd think you were crazy, on account of the number of times you've hung out there."

For some reason, knowing that Maddie didn't just ditch him for Eric made him feel loads better. Cornelious agreed it was a solid idea, and the duo met up with Pilot and Carly and revealed Maddie's plan.

"Ugh. Just don't start talking to Mrs. Henry. She'll have your ear for hours," Carly warned.

27

"You know, you could've just asked someone."

"Ugh, Carly. For the trillionth time, I know. I just didn't feel like going to some dumb dance. Especially with the group you're all going with." Maddie explained, as she zippered up her jacket and grabbed her bookbag. "Besides, tonight I'm finally going to the Henry's to investigate. We have made no progress on the case for about two weeks now."

"You're obsessed," Carly stated as she finished straightening her hair. She got up from her cushion in front of the mirror and headed into her private bathroom to fish out some lipstick. After tossing aside different shades of pink, all of which looked indistinguishable from each other, she applied the perfect color.

"We're just so close I know it!" Maddie retorted and swung her backpack over her shoulder.

"Well---" Carly was interrupted when her mom shouted from downstairs that the boys were here.

Maddie quickly helped a nervous Carly tie her pink halter-top dress, and the two headed down the wooden staircase. Downstairs, in the foyer, the boys were waiting. Pilot was nervously holding a bunch of flowers, and Cornelious was casually talking to Carly's parents. Maddie came down the stairs first, not wanting to ruin Carly's 'entrance'. Embarrassingly, when Pilot saw Carly he quickly dropped down on one knee (not really sure what to do). Cornelious swiftly pulled Pilot back up beside him, causing both Mr. and Mrs. Cosentino to chuckle. However, they composed themselves immediately after a glare from their youngest.

"Well, aren't you guys just precious?" Mr. Cosentino said, clicking off some pictures.

"Oh, Madeline. Where's your date?" Mrs. Cosentino asked, concerned. "You're not getting stood up are you?"

"Mom!"

"You can't get stood up, if you were never asked, Mrs. Cosentino," Alexis replied, as she smiled sweetly and hung onto Cornelious' shoulder. Cornelious shrugged as Maddie rolled her eyes at his horrible choice of a date.

Carly stuck up for her bud and told her parents, "Actually, the girls ask the guys to this one. Plus, Maddie has other plans tonight."

Before Mrs. Cosentino could play twenty questions,

Maddie waved goodbye, and biked to the easternmost part of town, right down the block from the entrance to the Gibbz's grounds. The Henry's loved to showboat their wealth, and had placed three feet of golden block letters spelling: HENRY on the grassy area between the street and sidewalk next to the mailbox--- or road verge, as Maddie had discovered, after researching the name for it back in middle school. Sighing, Maddie drove up the winding driveway, and parked her bike in their official Tour de France bike-rack. Walking up to the Henry door, she prayed Eric would answer instead of his mother, for Mrs. Henry's chatty-reputation had always preceded her.

Before Maddie could even place her finger on the doorbell, the huge wooden doors swung open, and Mrs. Henry stood before her with a large yellow lily in her hair, donning a flowery apron, and holding a tray of mouth-watering homemade (or rather maid-made) flower cookies. "Do come in, darling."

"Thanks," Maddie had the creeping feeling that this was going to be a long night.

"Now why didn't either of you attend that little school dance tonight? You could still go, there's plenty of time. I can buy a dress for you in no time. It's really no imposition at all. And Eric does look so handsome in formal wear, and no, that's not just a mother's opinion. Cookie?"

Already Maddie was lost. "Sure, thanks. Where's---"

"Eric? Oh, he'll be down shortly. Don't you worry. Follow me, I'll give you a tour of the house." At first, Maddie was excited and attentive as Mrs. Henry toured the mansion. But after thirty-six minutes had elapsed, Mrs. Henry was basically pulling Maddie from room to room. Finally, they turned a corner and entered a small den with various paintings and woodworks exhibited along the walls. "Most of these were actually done by Eric himself. He's quite the little artist. You see that that rocking chair over there with the initials E.H. and R.S.? Well, he just finished that beauty in woodshop about two months ago. Impressive, right?"

"Mom! I've been looking for you two for half an hour!" Eric interrupted, as he threw open the doors to the den.

"Sorry, hon. We're two chatty Kathys, aren't we? It was a pleasure talking to you. Let's do this again, just us girls," Mrs. Henry winked, as she turned and spun out of the den.

"I hope she didn't talk too much," Eric blushed and walked over towards Maddie.

"Huh? Sorry, I think I'm deaf now," Maddie joked, which helped break up the awkward atmosphere.

Eric smiled and the two headed over to the desk in the middle of the room, where papers and utensils were stacked neatly in bins. Maddie stifled a laugh at the impressive array of oil pastels and canvases placed on the table. She had figured they would make a rough sketch on computer paper, because for once Maddie could care less about winning this contest. Eric, on the other hand, wasted no time and shared his ideas on the project.

****

Meanwhile, in the Asbury High gymnasium, students were

admiring the Spring Fling decorations (thanks to the donations to the booster club from generous East Asbury families). Flowers of every color popped out of the walls, and hung from the rafters. Although the dance floor was still the laminate gymnasium floor, the surrounding floor area was covered with a green substance, that appeared and felt more like grass than actual carpet. On the walls, lavender, blue, and pink lights lit up the gym, leaving students feeling as if they were outside admiring a wonderful sunset. But the best aspect of the dance was that the school had relented and for once had agreed to actually hire a DJ, rather than use a teacher. And yes, the students were pumped.

The hallway outside of the gymnasium was lined with three long tables, smothered in chips, drinks, and desserts (Mr. Caulfield did make some candies, but the seniors had immediately made sure to scrape up every last morsel). Additionally, it was out in the hallway that the teachers chose to chaperone, rather than stand in the gym and watch the students dance. Students liked this arrangement better too, for the teachers' comments on the appropriate way to dance were as annoying as they were endless.

"So...do you want to dance?" Alexis was pulling Cornelious to the dance floor, and looking over to where Carly and Pilot were dancing, in their own little world.

Even though Cornelious had agreed to go to the Fling with Alexis, he hated dancing. He just figured everyone else would be going, and he might as well make an appearance.

Crap, Cornelious realized, I can't believe I thought I

should make an appearance. I'm turning into my dad! Reflecting on how much his dad had loved that he had attended the dance with Alexis suddenly repulsed him. Abruptly, Cornelious needed some air, and broke away from Alexis.

"I'm sorry...I, er, I'm just not the dancing-type."

Cornelious turned and walked into the hallway, but heard Alexis complain, "THEN WHY DID YOU SAY YES?! I COULD HAVE WENT WITH A SOPHMORE!"

After hearing Alexis yelling across the gymnasium, Carly looked up and saw that Cornelious was leaving. "Pi?"

"Yeah?" Pilot took a chance and took his eyes off of the floor---when it came to dancing, he was the Godzilla of destroying feet.

"I think Cornelious is leaving...and he's our ride."

"Oh," Pilot was disappointed. As bad as he was at dancing, he was enjoying whirling Carly around, as well as the jealous looks he garnered from his peers.

"Don't worry, Pi. They'll be other dances," Carly quickly kissed Pilot. It always seemed as if the two were so in-sync that they could sense each other's feelings, which is why no one understood what took so long for the two to get together.

"NEAL! WAIT UP!" Carly bellowed. The trio met up outside the gymnasium doors, and agreed to go back to Pilot's and wait for word from Maddie.

"Hey, guys look. I think Caulfield has the hots for Clarke," Pilot pointed to where the two were laughing behind the dessert table.

"Well, she is wearing some nice jewelry... I bet he bought it for her with the money he's getting from the Food Network! Isn't that cute?!" Carly looked at both boys, who blankly stared at her. "I seriously need some more girl friends," Carly murmured as the limo pulled up and the gang headed westward laughing.

****

"Oh, hey kids," Ms. Owens yawned as she wrenched open the door. "Maddie just arrived...she's upstairs...waiting." Ms. Owens arched her eyebrows at Pilot.

When Ms. Owens said 'waiting' she literally meant waiting, outside Pilot's room. The Owens may not have been rich, but Pilot knew how to buy, sell, save, and invent. Each of these four interests, helped fund Pilot's tech-addiction. In order to get into his room, or fortress (as it was deemed), one had to key in a five-digit code, next to the titanium door, on a keypad that was concealed under what appeared to be an outlet. Once the code was typed in, Pilot installed voice-activation software where he only had to say, "LIONS" in order to unlock the door. Yes, Pilot's room had a bed, closet, and dresser on one side, but those are the only aspects of the room that identify it as a bedroom. On the far side of the room, a desk was situated in which two laptops were plugged into a desktop. On the wall behind the desk was a giant flatscreen plugged into the desktop. Therefore, any of the information from any of the computers could be easily viewed on the flatscreen. Next to the window facing Maddie's room, was a recently purchased smartboard, which displayed codes and formulas (that only made sense to Pilot), as well as the thief's pattern.

Various cables, old mouses, hard-drives, dusty computer batteries, and other various tools of technology covered the floor. The gang made sure to sidestep every piece---years ago, Cornelious had accidentally cracked an old mouse and still wasn't sure if Pilot had forgotten or even forgiven him.

"Watch out guys, I haven't had a chance to clean. Cornelious, try not to step on anything---be extra vigilant."

Apparently, Pilot had neither forgotten nor forgiven, and instructed the threesome to sit on his bed as he went over the pattern again on his smartboard. After some discussion, and Maddie's retelling of the grand tour she experienced from Mrs. Henry---which caused some much-needed laughter---the gang felt exhausted from their long night. As Carly, Maddie, and Cornelious were drifting to sleep in Pilot's bed, with Pilot following suit in his chair, Carly suddenly sprung up and successfully stirred everyone awake.

"Guys! I know when the next theft is!"

"WHAT?!"

"HOW?!"

"HUH?!"

Another positive aspect of Pilot's room was his sound-proof walls, for Ms. Owens would have definitely been pulled out of her much-needed sleep at their cries of excitement.

"The second weekend in April!"

"That's in two weeks, Car. How could you possibly know

that?" Maddie skeptically questioned.

"Because, it's the date in which your parents, AND the Help, will definitely one hundred percent be out of the house!" Carly exclaimed proudly.

"How could you possibly know that?"

"Honestly, Neal how do you not? Remember at the Christmas Ball, your dad was telling anyone who would listen about the international business meeting in Versailles? He was extra excited because that's where your parents' honeymoon was---which is way cute that he was excited, by the way---and Jason asked if you were going, but your dad said no AND that no one's going to be in the house that weekend because that you'll be staying at Eric's...which really means you're probably staying at Maddie's right? I mean why stay----"

"Car, you're rambling now," Pilot interrupted, but when he noticed Carly cross her arms angrily, he quickly stated, "But she's right. I remember hearing that. And I remember Mr. Wallabee saying that he and his wife were out dancing at the Halloween Ball, so that no one was home during their theft either."

"I bet if we double-checked---"

"Which is what we have to do," Maddie cut in.

"If we double checked," Carly continued, ignoring her friend, "We will find that no one was home at any of the houses after the robber settled in, and found a decent hiding spot. So, he only had to wait until everyone left their mansions to do as he pleased."

Even though the gang didn't completely agree with Carly's logic, they agreed to test her theory, and try to catch the robber in the act exactly two weeks from tonight. For now, the gang had to wait and hope the thief wouldn't strike before then. After all, the one thing the gang did agree on is that the Gibbz theft was sure to be the last.

28

As March ended and April began, the atmosphere in Asbury High changed drastically. Teachers noticed many students came to school dressed nicer, and there were virtually no quarrels or fights in the school. New teachers thought there was simply something in the air, seasoned professionals realized that the Prom was fast approaching and those left unasked were trying their best to change their luck. Furthermore, with the Prom looming in the distance, a large number of students were seen cozying up to each other--- however, after Prom weekend about ninety percent of theses couples would go back to being singles.

With all the drama and rumors flying around in regards to Prom, Carly found herself actually enjoying school. At their lunch table, the gang was now joined by Heather, Peetie, and Nya (luckily, Alexis was still upset at being left at the Spring Fling and didn't want to sit anywhere near Cornelious).

"Yes, but I heard Andi had already said yes to John, but now John wants to go with Kristen," Peetie gushed.

"No no no. John asked Andi, but she said no, so he asked Kristen, but now Andi changed her mind because she's jealous of Kristen," Carly explained.

Heather, Nya, and Peetie all shook their head in understanding and began discussing some more information. Cornelious, Pilot, and Maddie slid down the table a little more, and talked about other any topic that crossed their mind.

"I heard James Wilson wanted to ask you, Carly," Heather stated looking at Pilot.

"What?!" Pilot turned around to join the conversation. Maddie and Cornelious decided they didn't want to listen to Carly say she had no intention of going with him, only to have Pilot make a commotion out of nothing, ending in both of them angry at each other. Instead, they began their own conversation.

"What time are you coming over tonight? My mom's all excited and made a big dinner for you," Maddie explained taking a chunk out of her peanut butter and jelly sandwich.

Cornelious drained his milk and replied, "Well, my parents are leaving at 4ish, so I'll be there at 5... What time is dinner, because aren't we planning on reconnaissance?"

"Reconnaissance?" she laughed.

"You know, spying? Investigating?

"Yeah, yeah. I know what reconnaissance means, it's just funny you chose that word."

"Well, this is serious. It's my house now," Cornelious blushed.

"You're right, I'm sorry. Really," Maddie composed herself and added, "Well, we usually eat around five, five-thirty. So maybe we'll head over to your place around six-thirty or seven."

"Cool. Are we going to meet up with them there," Cornelious began indicating Pilot and Carly who were now yelling at each other, "or tell them to come to your house?"

"I'll just tell them to meet at my house a little after six."
****

Honestly, after the delectable meal of pot roast, string beans, and mashed potatoes, Maddie and Cornelious could barely make it up to Maddie's room. Therefore, it was simply unfathomable that they were able to climb their way out of Maddie's window and meet up with Pilot and Carly below.

"Ugh, I'm stuffed," Maddie complained.

"Me too. We better not eat like this every night."

"Quit complaining and get moving. The thief may have already struck!" Pilot urged.

Knowing he was right, the gang jumped on their bikes and hurriedly sped their way to the Gibbz's.

"Okay we know that if the thief is there he, or she, must've used the cat prop and asked Charlene to let him in. If Charlene wasn't so forgetful we could ask her," Carly began.

Cornelious shook his head, "We couldn't even ask her if we wanted… she left as soon as my parents left and is pretty much scared of anyone under eighteen. She won't even look me in my eyes, so I highly doubt she'd remember what the thief looked like, let alone have enough courage to hold a conversation with me for long enough to describe him… or her."

Carly finally understood why the brown-haired maid was always running away from her when she came over. Breathing out slowly she continued, "Okay… weird, but whatever… and anyway, how in the world is the thief going to be able to get away? There are two gates he has to get by, and the first one is voice activated, right?" Carly asked as they approached the first gate.

"I was thinking the same thing... but you did mention that my dad gave everyone off for the weekend, so I guess Mike has off too. My dad's so cocky he probably figured no one would dare rob a Gibbz," Cornelious rolled his eyes.

"Okay, then it's possible to get past the second gate, but that still doesn't explain how to get by the voice-activated first gate. Especially, if Mike's not here to check that the voice matches the person, and then press the button to let them in," Maddie pointed out.

The gang realized they had no sure answer of how the thief could escape, but figured they should try to catch him before he had a chance to flee. When they reached the fountain, they turned right and went around the side. As a precaution, Pilot and Cornelious had placed a ladder against the house that led into a second-floor window. It was decided earlier that busting in through the front door would draw unnecessary attention, and possibly scare the thief away before they could find him.

After ensuring that the ladder was sturdy, Maddie, Cornelious, Carly, and Pilot silently made their way up the ladder and into the second-floor guest room. No one spoke as they carefully tip-toed around the bed, past the Cherry Aspen combo dresser, and over to the door. Before heading into this venture, they had all decided it would be more prudent not to speak aloud. Thus, they used very basic hand gestures to signal when to stop and when to keep moving, and in what direction.

Cornelious reached the doorway first and slowly stuck his head out. After sensing no danger, he motioned for the other three to come join him in the hallway. With everyone in the hallway, they all stood still and strained to make sure they didn't miss a sound. They silently edged forward until they reached the top of the staircase.

Maddie slid over to Cornelious and started to gesture that they should slowly make their way downstairs, when she thought she heard a door opening or closing. The only problem was, it sounded like it was coming from behind them. Apparently, Cornelious had heard it too, for he slowly turned and raised the flashlight over to where Carly was nervously playing with her nails. Standing right behind Carly, raising a dangerous-looking object above his head, was a figure clad in all black, without an inch of skin showing.

Immediately, all three knew it was the thief. Carly was literally the only one left in the dark.

Although Maddie and Cornelious had heard the noise and turned around first, Pilot was the first one to spring into action. As the thief began to swing his weapon, Pilot lunged forward and knocked Carly to the ground.

"Ouch! What the---," but Carly cut herself short as she realized what had taken place. Pilot had pushed her out of the way and ended up leaving himself totally vulnerable to the thief. Before anyone could make a move, the thief swung his weapon at Pilot and instantly made contact. As Pilot crumpled to the ground, Maddie and Cornelious lunged at the thief. Using only his body, he bowled over Cornelious and threw his weapon at Maddie---who luckily ducked down in time.

"Neal! You okay?" Maddie asked rushing over to his side.

"Yeah, fine. Let's go! He's getting away!" Cornelious sprang up and ran down the stairs in pursuit of the thief.

Before joining him, Maddie ran to where Pilot lay unconscious. She, thankfully, felt a pulse and ordered Carly to call 911 immediately. Carly wiped away her tears and dug her phone out of her pocket. Not wanting to waste any more time Maddie sprinted down the staircase, and into the den, to the left of the main door.

To Maddie, it looked like a fight scene ripped out of a badly choreographed movie. Cornelious had temporarily stopped the thief from leaving out the far side window in the den. The thief was holding a bulging bag (full of stolen goods) in one hand, and a poker he had grabbed from the fireplace in the other. The only thing between the thief and Cornelious was the leather couch and stained wooden coffee table. However, the only thing between Maddie and the thief was, well nothing. Cornelious realized this too, and tried to distract the thief by keeping his full attention.

"So you're pretty tough... strong.... fast," Cornelious said as he kept shifting left and right to keep the thief cornered. "Did you ever play football?"

Apparently, this proved to be the wrong thing to say. The thief stopped moving and completely stiffened up. Hence, he heard Maddie moving behind him. Before anyone could make a move, the thief hit Maddie across the stomach with the poker and kicked her against the wall.

"NO!" Cornelious yelled as he tackled the thief and landed some punches on his chest. Unfortunately, the thief was stronger and able to maneuver his way out of Cornelious' grasp. Cornelious managed to get up quickly, but received a straight punch to the nose. Hearing his nose crack, Cornelious dived and grabbed the thief's legs. The thief stumbled for a second, but freed himself by kicking Cornelious in the face, leaving him no choice but to give up the fight.

Maddie, although pretty sure she had cracked or at least bruised her rib cage, staggered up and attempted to fight the thief. Laughing, the thief swung at Maddie. She dodged the first two punches, but the third one connected on her jaw and she fell back, yet again. Cornelious, blinded by his bloody and definitely broken nose, tried to stand up, but discovered his legs felt like jello.

Realizing they had been beat, they watched as the thief threw the bag of stolen goods out of the window and followed suite. Too tired and too sore to follow, the two pulled themselves up onto the couch and collapsed. About four minutes after the thief fled, Maddie and Cornelious heard the cop sirens and hoped that maybe they had caught the thief fleeing the premises---although they figured that was highly unlikely.

"My dad's gonna be pissed there's blood all over this couch," Cornelious laughed.

"At least it's not mine. Or he'd probably have you arrested too."

"GUYS! Pilot's coming to!" Carly exclaimed from upstairs.

Maddie and Cornelious considered that maybe they were lucky after all. Considering that no one had gotten killed or anything. But after the cops burst through the door, led by an angry Officer Chip, Cornelious and Maddie reconsidered their luck.

29

As if warning the gang to stay away from the investigation, or face jail time for obstruction of justice was not embarrassing enough, the police had decided to humiliate them even further. After hearing each of their stories, Officers Tennett and Swanson had called their parents. The Cosentinos thought it was cute they had tried to catch the thief, but warned Carly later about the dangerous undertaking of such a task. Ms. Owens was embarrassed, but was relieved that Pilot had only suffered a mild concussion and would remain in fine health. The Petrozzas yelled until their voices were stretched thinner than a contortionist doing the limbo. However, because Maddie knew better than to argue, they relented and only grounded her for a measly weekend. Obviously, Cornelious had received the biggest punishment from his parents. Although his mother's first question was whether Howie was harmed in the scuffle (as she called the robbery), Cornelious was shocked to see how worried his mom was over his well-being, and ended up giving him two weeks of grounding. Jeremiah Gibbz laughed at this decree and declared that Cornelious is to receive a two-month grounding AND he must ask permission first before having any friends over in the future. Jeremiah had also recommended plastic surgery to fix Cornelious' bruised and broken nose, but Cornelious had simply gotten up and acted as if he hadn't heard the suggestion. Let's just say Cornelious didn't tell Pilot, Maddie, or Carly about the last part of this conversation.

A month after the Gibbz robbery, the police were stumped---as Pilot learned from their case files. In fact, most citizens believed that since the Gibbz robbery was the largest amount totaling 113,000 dollars, the thief had probably skipped town and decided to pick up elsewhere. Even though it was rumored Jeremiah Gibbz had contacted the FBI, no new leads or suspects were being considered. Nevertheless, the gang still met up when they could and continued to fruitlessly review the case.

Hence, Pilot and Maddie found themselves biking to Brady's to meet up with Cornelious and Carly. The fact that tonight was Asbury High's beloved Prom made it easier to have a quiet conversation at Brady's. Most people were either getting ready for the big dance, or eagerly standing by the main entrance to the Luxurious Lady (where the Prom was held), to watch the famous red-carpet walk-in. Because Pilot and Maddie were riding their bikes from their houses, they found themselves en route to pass the Luxurious Lady.

As they passed the low-income Vin-Jak condominiums and neared Split Park, across from the Luxurious Lady, Pilot stopped to complain, "Look how crowded it is! Can't we just cut back to the skate park, and enter the boardwalk from behind the rides?"

"For the zillionth time, no. They blocked off the road to the left of the park, see?" Maddie pointed to the far end of the park and Pilot saw the line of trolleys, limos, and cars waiting to drop off their excited guests. Pilot agreed it would be best to continue their path and cut across the park to get to Brady's. Sighing, he turned on his bike and was about to peddle, when he noticed Maddie was staring over to where she had just instructed Pilot to look.

"Maddie, I get it. You were right. Let's go. Unless your ribs still hurt and you need to take a break."

"Ssshh! I'm thinking. And I'm fine, it was just a bad bruise, Cornelious has the broken nose."

"I know, I know...so, what are you thinking about?" Pilot asked as he realized Maddie had stopped listening and was squinting at a figure leaning against the trees. Although Maddie was staring pretty intently at the person, Pilot could tell that the person was clearly unaware.

"Pi, do you know who that is?" Maddie whispered, pointing at the figure.

"No..." Pilot squinted harder and edged forward a little.

"Oh yeah, it's Rodney Shiffler, right?"

"Ssshh not so loud!" Maddie warned.

"What? Why?"

"Why would Rodney Shiffler---guaranteed Prom King---not attend his Prom?" Maddie asked more to herself than Pilot, who only shrugged. "You'd think he have a date---seeing as he has been flying through girls this year," Maddie stated, quoting Carly and her brother.

"True, but they all seemed pretty pissed at him," Pilot remembered the angry girls in school or Brady's or just about anywhere.

"Yeah, they were really upset with him. Carly even mentioned his exes saying he always seemed distracted, as if he could really care less about them...Almost as if it were for appearances sake..."

"Girls always think that, but they don't realize the effort us guys---"

Ignoring Pilot and trying to allow her words to catch up with her thoughts, Maddie continued to think aloud, "He IS an athlete too, which makes him fast and strong. And at the Gibbz's break-in Cornelious had mentioned something about the thief playing football---which we thought confused him, because he stiffened up. BUT what if he really IS a football player and thought for a second that we recognized him? That would make anyone freeze up, right?"

"Uh..."

"AND---how did we NOT see this before?!---he IS a member of woodshop class. In fact, I remember Eric pointing out they were partners for some project, after I mentioned the carved initials on some rocking chair in his house! So, he had plenty of free access to sandpaper, and I know for a fact that he had Cat as a teacher, because Trent was in his class and Rodney was always asking him for help. Plus, he's been acting so strange this year!" Maddie's voice was rising in excitement.

"He has been acting differently this year. I mean I don't personally know him, but I know he used to be in the Honor Society and got kicked out---he was supposed to talk to my math class about the importance of school earlier this year, but Mrs. Endidoto said he was no longer a member and we had to take a pop quiz that day instead and I---"

"Pilot! Focus!"

"Sorry."

"Okay, so I think we're in agreement?"

"Well...we still need evidence."

Maddie thought hard for a second and came up with a resolution. "Okay, you head to Brady's and tell Cornelious and Carly about the newest development. I'm going to follow Rodney home and see if I can find anything suspicious."

"No way! You're not going alone. I'll come with you."

"No. You have to tell the others," Maddie looked over her shoulder and saw that Rodney had turned and appeared to be leaving, "I have to go. Now. If you don't hear from me in an hour, er, go to Rodney's."

"What if he turns homicidal and chops you into pieces or something?"

Maddie looked at Pilot and laughed, "He's a thief. Not a murderer."

As Maddie turned her bike and snuck away to follow Rodney, Pilot swallowed his fear and sped off to Brady's to tell the gang.

****

No matter how easy it looks on TV, following somebody back to their house without being spotted is difficult. Maddie thought for sure that Rodney had seen her a few times, but after each pause he would continue on his way. After six blocks, Rodney stopped outside his white-picket fence and swung the gate wide open. Making sure she wasn't seen, Maddie quickly made it through the gate before it closed and successfully hid behind the bushes that lined the fence. With the sun slowly setting, there was enough light to see Rodney check his watch and creep silently around his house to a small toolshed. Carefully looking both ways (to ensure that the coast was clear), Rodney unlocked the door, and stepped inside.

Knowing it was now or never, Maddie counted to ten Mississippi, before following suite. However, once she stepped inside, she realized a small trap door in the floor was propped open, with a wooden staircase leading into a dark basement. Hoping Rodney would be too preoccupied to hear her footfalls, Maddie began her descent. As she reached the dirt ground, she crept along the walls, and remained in semi-darkness. Clearly, Rodney had built this hideout himself. The staircase was probably easy for someone in woodshop,

Maddie mused. And the rest of the basement was really just a dirt floor with dirt walls. The only piece of furniture was a beat-up grey couch to the right of the staircase, and a long wooden table in the back of the room. Currently, Rodney was standing with his back to the staircase (and therefore Maddie), and was leaning on the table, where all of the stolen goods were situated. Splayed across the table, right out in the open, there were piles of assorted jewelry, cash, and even a few paintings. Maddie knew that this was all the evidence they needed, and desperately wished for a camera, or that her friends would hurry up. Looking down, she checked her wristwatch and felt the desire to bang her head against the wall. She stupidly told Pilot to wait an hour when only eighteen minutes had passed! Before she could continue berating herself, Maddie recognized that Rodney was talking on his cell to someone.

"Yes, yes it's all here!... uh huh...I know...Now we can stand under those lights together counting our fortune!" Apparently, the the other person---his accomplice, Maddie believed---had said something funny, for Rodney had begun to laugh like a lunatic. "Reno is the perfect place for a new start!"

As Rodney continued to laugh, Maddie began to get the creeps. Thinking back on Pilot's last warning was enough to send Maddie shuffling along the wall, and back to the staircase. Suddenly, she felt a brush by her foot and heard an annoying "meow." One meow was all it took for Rodney to turn off his cell, spin around, and realize he had been discovered.

"Madeline Petrozza?"

"Er, it's Maddie," Maddie corrected him, and tried to take a backwards step up the staircase.

Unfortunately, Rodney was quicker. "What are you DOING HERE?!" Before giving her time to respond, Rodney grabbed Maddie by the right arm and pulled her over to the table. Realizing things had just taken a turn for the worse, Maddie used her free arm to wind up and hit Rodney across the face. Startled, he let go of Maddie's sleeve, and she wasted no time sprinting to the staircase. When Maddie had made it halfway up the stairs, Rodney lunged and tackled her, sending her back down to the dirt floor. Using her arms (and face) to brace her fall, Maddie's only strength was left in her legs. Rodney maintained a tight grip around her lower half, leaving her with little room to kick him as hard as she could manage. After a well-aimed kick, she made contact with his face and squirmed free.

For most people, that kick would have allowed Maddie time to make her way up the stairs and escape. But filled with adrenaline and the knowledge that he was caught, Rodney fought back the pain, punched her in the back of the head, and---for good measure---kicked her as she fell back to the floor. Maddie used what little strength she could muster to crawl towards the staircase. She tried to call out for help, but the thick mixture of dirt and blood choked back any sound that rose in her throat. Rodney flipped her over and, grabbing her by the front of her t-shirt, brought his hand back to strike her. Closing her eyes to brace herself, she heard a voice remark, "this looks familiar," and looked up to see Cornelious jump off the staircase and tackle Rodney to the ground. Allowing him no time to recover, Cornelious quickly punched Rodney in the face, and called up the stairs for help. In less than ten seconds, the whole Asbury Police force rushed down the stairs and pointed their weapons at Rodney. Knowing it was all over, Rodney held up his hands, strutted over to Officer Chip, and in one last act of defiance, spat in his face. Chip calmly wiped away the spit and ordered for 'the criminal' to be taken upstairs.

During all this commotion, Cornelious had rushed over to Maddie and half-carried her up the stairs. "Why am I always saving you from getting beat up?"

"I was...already beat up...when you...when you got here," Maddie exhaustingly countered.

"Still, at least you're breathing," Cornelious half-joked as he sat Maddie down on the curb in front of the Shiffler's. Looking over his friend's battered condition, he silently cursed himself for not coming sooner. He should never have listened to Pilot's advice to wait a whole freakin' hour! After ten minutes of anxiously pacing around inside Brady's, he had his driver pick them up, and stop at the police station. At first, no one made a move. But when Cornelious grabbed the limo driver's keys and sped off to the Shiffler's, the whole police station went haywire. Naturally, the Asbury Police force followed in pursuit of a 'crazy-spoiled-rich-unlicensed-driver.' Good thing for all parties involved that they did.

"Ahh...yeah. And this was...my favorite shirt...at least we.... we solved the case," Maddie smiled and began to close her eyes.

Not exactly knowing the rules of concussions, Cornelious quickly called for a medic and sat down next to Maddie, instructing her to keep talking and to keep her eyes open.

"I'm too tired...to talk," for the life of her, Maddie couldn't understand why everyone wanted to talk now. Cornelious, Pilot, and Carly all knew what happened. Surely, they could explain it to the cops. Plus, Maddie hated cops. They didn't care the first time she offered to help, but now they hung on every word she spoke, or managed to speak. When Cornelious sat down next to her, she leaned her head on his shoulder and tried to fall asleep.

"No, Mads. Wake up."

Quickly, the medic came over, and carried Maddie into the ambulance. By this time, Carly and Pilot had arrived. Cornelious and Pilot stayed behind to give statements, while Carly insisted on heading to the hospital with Maddie.

Luckily, with tonight being the Prom, the citizens of Asbury were busy fussing over other things. Believing their son was busy enjoying himself, the Shifflers were out dining in East Asbury's famous dessert parlor: Tyler's Tantalizing Treats. Unfortunately for the Shifflers, they found nothing sweet upon arriving home.

30

Naturally, the biggest news in school that week was not
the Prom. For once no one mentioned who wore what, or
even who won Prom King or Queen. Instead, all the
attention was focused on four freshmen, who were nowhere
near the Prom that night. Carly and Pilot may have been able
to slip by unnoticed, for only Cornelious and Maddie were
visibly injured, if it wasn't for Jason Scott repeating what his
sister had told him.

Although Carly loved the attention, after three days of
constant questioning and students flocking to her side, she
was ready to scream. Pilot stayed near Carly as often as he
could, so he was lucky to have her speak for the both of
them, and wasn't too bothered by the attention.

Also fortunate was the fact that Cornelious and Maddie

had every class together. They made sure to have each other's back---literally too, seeing as Maddie needed the extra help carrying her backpack, and other small tasks. Cornelious was amazed Maddie had come to school this week at all, if he was that beat up, he would have milked it for the rest of the year for sure.

"Finals are coming up," Maddie would mutter, when people would ask why she came to school.

Alexis indicated her injuries were only for attention, and tried to steer away any conversation consisting of Maddie's bravery, back to herself. Even Hannah had gotten fed up with Alexis, and sat with the gang at lunch for a few days.

By Friday the excitement died down, and the students were back to focusing on more trivial matters. Some people even mentioned dress choices at the Prom. In study hall, after making sure that no one had wanted to question them or talk about the robberies, Maddie voiced a nagging question that had been bugging her since that night.

"Guys, the investigation isn't over."

Carly pushed her book aside, and looked up, "We caught Rodney, got the glory, and people retrieved most of their money or stuff back. Seriously, what's left?"

Pilot shrugged, but Cornelious thought that whatever Maddie had to say would prove to be much more intriguing than his Economics assignment, so he stuck up for her. "Just let her explain."

Clearing her throat, she recounted Rodney's phone message. "He had to have had an accomplice. Am I right?"

Bitterly, Carly had to admit Maddie was correct, "Ugh, so what should we do?"

After considering this for a moment, Pilot whipped out his cell and started frantically typing. He explained that he had pulled up every file on Rodney that Asbury High had available, in hopes of finding a note or any information of an acquaintance. "Dang it! I thought that the guidance office would have something, anything really, to point us in the right direction. But I got nothing."

Carly recognized that Pilot was upset that his electronic search had yielded no successful results, so she tried to cheer him up. "Good try Pilot. How'd you manage to figure out the passwords?"

"It's pretty easy, if you think about it..." Pilot was already cheering up though, "Ms. Dugan's password is obviously CATS---the Broadway play she headlined. And Ms. Clarke's password is obviously RENO---she's obsessed with that place. And Coste's password is obviously---"

"WAIT! What did you say?" Maddie rose from her seat, excited.

"Which part?" Pilot asked confused.

"The accomplice, it's so obvious!" Maddie exclaimed, and grabbed Pilot's phone to dial 911.

"What are you doing, you can't call the police in school...can you?" Carly asked exasperated.

Cornelious grabbed Maddie and asked what they all wanted to know, "Who's the accomplice?"

Maddie looked at her friends and smiled. "Our favorite

new guidance counselor…Ms. Clarke! She is obsessed with Reno---the sign in her room 'The Biggest Little City in the World' and all those glittery snowglobes---they are obvious clues that we missed! But Pilot… how did you know she was obsessed with Reno?"

Pilot looked sheepish and said, "Well, I never got a guidance slip, unlike you three who were getting them like candy---"

"So she could figure out how to scapegoat my mom, while finding out what treasures you guys had in your houses!" Maddie explained.

"Yeah…but I didn't know that…so, I snuck into her office one day. I thought of Reno right away because of that hilarious show on comedy central," Pilot boasted.

"And Rodney did seem to be around her a lot this year, he was always walking in or out of the office when I would get called in," Cornelious realized. "She must be the accomplice."

The gang discussed the best course of action and called Officer Chip to let him know what they were thinking. Officer Chip replied that though he wished they would stay out of the investigation, since they were right about Rodney and led the police to the stolen goods, he had no choice but to believe them. Plus, he reasoned, with the old Chief retiring, this could lead to a serious promotion for him.

It was decided that while he would question Rodney at the station, acting as if they had caught his accomplice (hopefully scaring him into giving her up), the foursome would try to divulge more information from Ms. Clarke herself. Knowing it could be dangerous, Chip sent his two 'best and brightest officers'--- Swanson and Tennett. To ensure Ms. Clarke wouldn't spot them, get spooked, and possibly leave town, the officers would enter through the gymnasium around the back, and wait in the hallway outside the office.

After everything was sorted out, the gang got up and headed across the hall to Ms. Clarke's office. Her back was to the four of them when they walked in, and she appeared a little startled when she realized she had guests.

"Well, this is strange. Usually it's only one student at a time. What's wrong children?"

Maddie crossed her arms and said, "I'm a little shaken up from recent events."

"Ah. I understand," Ms. Clarke took her seat, and nodded in empathy. Or rather faux empathy.

"But I don't, not really. How does an average-minded student become such a criminal mastermind?"

"I wouldn't say mastermind. He did get caught," Carly added.

"Okay, well how did Rodney manage to think of a plan clever enough to break-in undetected into each house?" Cornelious interjected.

Ms. Clarke shook her head sadly, "Children, children. How am I supposed to know? Maybe we don't give his mind enough credit."

"Hmmm, I think we're not giving his heart enough credit..." Maddie stated.

"I don't follow," Ms. Clarke said, nodding her head in a

show of confusion.

"Seeing as Trent and Rodney were always on the same team, and occasionally hung out, my brother knows an awful lot about him. Apparently, when Rodney was 'in love' he would do anything his girlfriend wanted. And I mean anything. One time he bought his girlfriend a baby pig, after she mentioned her love for the movie Babe---that didn't go over too well. And we think he only started robbing houses, after being egged on by a new girlfriend," Maddie explained.

"And we think the girls he dated this year were only for appearances sake, so he could escape suspicion," Carly added smiling.

"And it was only after this year began, that Rodney started acting differently, so he must have met someone new this year. And for this special someone, we're guessing he would listen to anything she said and do whatever she wanted," Pilot resolved, and each member of the gang nodded in assent.

Ms. Clarke's demeanor was slowing changing. Although she thought she was playing it cool, the gang knew they were beginning to unnerve her.

"What I couldn't figure out was how Rodney got through that first gate at my house," Cornelious interjected. "But then I remembered that you asked permission to tape-record my sessions. So, Rodney clearly had my voice saying my name on tape, which enabled him to get past the gates." Cornelious figured this out on a whim, but Ms. Clarke believed he had hard evidence. Why else would they had entered her office so confidently?

"And, I must say, your obsession with Reno did you in," Maddie smugly added.

"How?" Ms. Clarke demanded, but then reconsidered, "I mean, what?"

"Look around. It's everywhere. Rodney couldn't keep his mouth shut about escaping with an older woman, and moving to her heart's desire---Reno," Maddie bluffed.

Unhinged, Ms. Clarke sprang up and told the kids, "Sure he was cute, but I should've known Rodney would behave like a stupid boy when he got caught!... I should've known he'd get caught..." She seemed to lose her train of thought for a moment. When she spoke again, a smile slowly crossed her face, "Now listen here, brats. You've got no real evidence, or the police would be here right?" As Ms. Clarke asked this, she spotted Officers Tennett and Swanson in the hallway, and collapsed onto the table, all traces of a smile were wiped from her face. "Okay, alright. I need a lawyer."

****

Not wanting to draw any more attention to themselves, the gang told Officers Swanson and Tennett to take all the credit for catching Ms. Clarke. Maddie even told them what to say to the media.

Of course, the following Monday Jason Scott had to rub it in Maddie's face that she had only solved half of the mystery and that the REAL police had solved the more important part. Maddie wanted to hit him, but instead said, "Who would've guessed a teacher would be guilty?"

"Obviously not you," Jason snickered.

Maddie turned and walked down the hallway to meet up with Cornelious, Pilot, and Carly. Though the school year had about two weeks left, the gang couldn't believe how quickly their first year of high school had passed.

Needless to say, they all knew that they would never forget their freshman year. Especially, with all the bruises and injuries they had sustained. When school ended that day, the gang headed to the beach to study for Finals and bask in the sun. Maddie, Cornelious, Pilot, and Carly watched as their classmates dove, ran, walked, and were tugged into the water. For some reason, each of them had the distinct feeling that this summer would be even more interesting than the school year had been. But, for now, the gang was content with taking it easy.

NOTE TO READER:

Thank you for reading. If you've enjoyed Asbury High and the Thief's Gamble, SPREAD THE WORD!

As an independent author, the best way to gain exposure and to keep more books coming, is for our fans to leave reviews. Of course, word of mouth and social media exposure is appreciated as well---but I'd love to read your thoughts on the book.

For upcoming books, more news and even to contact me directly, please visit my website at:

www.kbchannick.com

COMING SOON:

ASBURY HIGH
AND THE PARCELS OF POISON

BOOK TWO IN THE ASBURY HIGH SERIES

ABOUT THE AUTHOR

For as long as she could remember, Kelly Brady Channick loved making up stories, and leaving her listeners/readers on the edge of their seats.

Perhaps that's why she always managed to talk herself out of trouble...

After graduating from Ocean City High School, NJ, Kelly accepted a basketball scholarship to Holy Family University, in Philadelphia. As a lifelong athlete, Kelly understands the importance of teamwork and overcoming adversity, both of which she hopes translates into her books.

Before writing page-turners, she taught first, fifth, sixth, seventh and eighth grade — like a dessert menu, she simply had to test them all out. But her favorite job is the one she's now doing full time: writing. Kelly loves to craft whodunit mysteries, leading readers through various twists and turns, filled with red-herrings, hidden clues, and more peculiar characters than you'd find in a circus.

Kelly lives in South Jersey with her handsome husband, energetic baby boy, two cookie-stealing dogs, and an awfully smart cat.

If you want to know when Kelly's next book will come out, please visit her website at http://www.kbchannick.com.

Made in the USA
Middletown, DE
07 March 2020